JILL AND THE PERFECT PONY

Amanda Applewood has a perfect pony,
but she doesn't like riding. She has been
invited to stay with the Lockett family
and be a member of their team in a
gymkhana, but she can't be bothered
to go, and gets Jill to take her place. To
Jill's horror, the Locketts think she is
the impossible Amanda, and treat her
accordingly. And so Jill finds herself
riding in the gymkhana under another
name and on a borrowed pony.

**More 'Jill' stories
available in Knight Books**

Jill and the Perfect Pony

Ruby Ferguson

KNIGHT BOOKS
Hodder and Stoughton

Text copyright © 1959, 1993 Hodder
and Stoughton Ltd

First published by Hodder and
Stoughton Ltd 1959

This edition first published in 1969
by Knight Books
Revised edition 1993

ISBN 0 340 59079 3

Printed and bound in Great Britain
for Hodder and Stoughton Books, a
division of Hodder and Stoughton Ltd,
Mill Road, Dunton Green, Sevenoaks,
Kent TN13 2YA (Editorial Office: 47
Bedford Square, London WC1B 3DP)
by Cox & Wyman Ltd, Reading, Berks.
Typeset by Hewer Text Composition
Services, Edinburgh.

Contents

1 The Applewood girl

There was a girl living near us with a perfect pony, called Amanda Applewood. I mean the girl, not the pony. The pony's name was Plum, which I consider not only an insult but a very poor effort on the part of anybody who personally rejoices in such a mouthful as Amanda Applewood.

I had never seen Amanda ride, but Plum was a sort of legend in our neighbourhood. She was said to be fabulous, and never to put a foot wrong. None of us really knew Amanda, because she didn't belong to our crowd. She learned her riding at school, where she went as a weekly boarder. Plum had been selected and bought for her by her father – doubtless for some princely sum – and I cannot think of anything more dim than letting somebody else choose your pony, even if it's your own parent.

Nor did Amanda ride in our local events, because her mother said that wasn't the way to get to Wembley with Princess Anne handing you a silver cup.

By now you have probably got the impression that girl to girl, Amanda was a shocker, but that wasn't really so. She was quite a friendly type, only one didn't run into her much, going to a different school and so on.

It was the beginning of the summer holidays, and I was sitting on a gate in the lane, in a sort of happy trance. Mummy was away in London and likely to stay about a fortnight, as the BBC was making one of her children's books into a television serial and she wanted to be in at the murder, so to speak. She had tried to persuade me to go and stay with a friend, but I had pleaded that I was quite all right at home, and had won the day; so it had been arranged that an artist friend of Mummy's called Grace Webb should come and sleep at the cottage each night. I didn't mind Miss Webb at all. She was harmless and rather like her name, gracious and graceful in a sort of spiderish way, and usually she was so wrapped up in the world of art that she hardly spoke at all, which suited me, because conversationally I don't think we should ever have clicked. She arrived at the cottage every night about seven, and when I came in about nine we would have a cup of cocoa and some biscuits, and she would say very nicely, 'How are the ponies?' and I would say very politely, 'How's the art coming on?' and she would smile and so would I, and that was that. Nothing to object to at all, nor did she ever make boring remarks like, 'Are you sure your feet aren't wet?' I discovered that there's one thing that artists and horsy people have in common; they are above such things as wet feet, messy clothes, and keeping your bedroom drawers tidy, which makes life comfortable.

However, it was a Monday afternoon and I was sitting on this gate feeling a bit lazy and wondering what to do, when I saw Amanda Applewood strolling towards me along the lane.

I thought she would have gone right by, but to my surprise she said, 'Hello,' and stopped.

She was wearing a very tidy grey coat and skirt, a white blouse (clean) with a pink and green striped school tie, tights (fancy, on an ordinary afternoon!)

and actually gloves. I had on my oldest jodhs and a pretty awful sweater, as I had just emerged from a slight argument with Rapide who had developed a sudden strong objection to doing half-passes.

'Hello,' I said.

'I say,' said Amanda, 'you know all about ponies, don't you?'

'Well, not all,' I said, 'but a bit.'

'There's something wrong with my pony,' said Amanda. 'She's making an awful din and I wondered whether I ought to call the vet.'

'Colic?' I said hopefully.

'Oh, I don't think so. They roll and yell, don't they? She just stands still and bellows.'

I said, 'What does your father think?' and she said, 'Daddy and Mummy are both away, and the man who comes every day to do our horses has got the day off, and Plum *would* go wrong just when I'm on my own. I say, would you mind coming up and having a look at her, if you're not doing anything?'

I was quite intrigued at the idea of seeing Amanda's home and stables and everything, so I said I'd go. We got to a white five-barred gate, and went up a long, tidy gravel drive. In front of the house there was a large lawn, cut so fine that it looked as if it had been painted on the ground, and some flower-beds full of rich pink geraniums. The house itself was long and large, built of red brick with a big white portico which is a superior kind of porch. At the side were some very clean stables, and I remembered hearing that Amanda's father kept two hunters. Amanda opened the door of a loose box, and there inside stood Plum, neighing away like mad.

'She does it all the time,' said Amanda. 'Do you think she's gone bats?'

It was my first real view of the perfect pony. She was a very pretty grey, with a white mane and tail, and at first sight looked much too pretty to be any good, only running my practised eye over her I noticed that she had lovely lines, and flawless legs and neck, and a very good head.

'I'll tell you what *I'd* say was the matter with her,' I said. 'She's bored stiff. What do you do with her?'

'*Do* with her?' said Amanda stupidly.

'Do you take her out a lot, and have fun with her?'

'Oh gosh, no,' said Amanda. 'I'm not all that keen. I just keep her for showing.'

'Golly!' I said. 'How would you like to be just kept for showing?'

'It's boring just riding her about,' said Amanda, going pink. 'And anyway, the man washed her last night and said I wasn't to take her out in case she got dirty.'

I felt very sorry for Plum, who had stopped neighing as soon as she saw me, doubtless thinking, poor animal, that I was about to take her for a nice ride. I only wished I could. I would have loved to try her, and I was hoping by now that Amanda would suggest it, but she didn't.

'I might ride her round the paddock a bit after tea,' she said indifferently, 'if you think that's what she needs.'

I patted Plum's silken neck and said, 'Buck up, old girl, perhaps life will give you a break,' and went out into the yard.

'Come on in, and we'll have tea,' said Amanda, and quite willingly I followed her into the house. We went into a very smart room with film-starish curtains and lamps and things, and Amanda rang a bell, and in came a man in a white jacket.

'Oh, we want some tea,' said Amanda, 'and tons of hot buttered toast, and enough jam for the lot, and tell Mrs Googe not that beastly gooseberry, either apricot or strawberry, and the same cake I had yesterday with the cherries in, and some chocolate biscuits if I left any, I don't remember.'

'Very good, miss,' said the man, just like they do in films.

I was enormously intrigued by now, and enjoying myself very much though I thought I must be dreaming. But in came this colossal tea with everything complete, and we ate and ate, piggish though it may sound, and I wondered if Amanda went on like this every day or if it was just laid on to impress me.

'I know all about you,' said Amanda, licking the last bit of chocolate off her fingers. 'You're a pretty hot rider, aren't you?'

'Oh, I don't know,' I said modestly.

'Oh, yes, you are. Much better than me, anyway. I just sit and let Plum do everything, which nobody can call actually riding, but I feel good when I win which is nearly always. I do believe in being honest about these things. Of course Plum is super.'

'I'm sure she is,' I murmured, wishing with all my heart that I could try the perfect pony for myself.

'I'm feeling rather miserable today,' said Amanda. 'I'm in a bit of a spot.'

'Oh, how's that?'

'Well,' she said, biting her thumbnail, 'I'm supposed to be going away tomorrow for about a fortnight, and I loathe the idea.'

'I suppose it's to some ghastly relations,' I said sympathetically, 'where they treat you as if you were about six.'

'Oh no,' said Amanda. 'Not like that at all. These

are some people that Mummy knows, I've never seen them, but they live in the country and do nothing but ride. They want me to go and make up a team, whatever that means. I take a dim view. I think they're the sort of types who haul you out of bed at six o'clock in the morning, harping on about what a gorgeous day it is and look at the shining dew, and let's go for a ride before breakfast, when actually I loathe getting up before ten in the holidays. I mean, what are the holidays for?'

'If you really want that answered,' I said, 'I think the holidays are just meant for getting all the riding you can. That's how it strikes me.'

'There you are!' said Amanda, scratching her ankle gloomily. 'You're the right type for that sort of thing, and I'm not. You ought to be going to these Locketts instead of me. Life's so unfair. All I want is to be left in peace to mooch about and watch the television, and Mummy fixes up this ghastly visit for me. Honestly, it'll kill me, I can't think of anything worse. Does your mother do things like that to you?'

'Occasionally,' I said. 'But as it happens she's away. I can do exactly as I like for a whole fortnight, it's wonderful.'

Amanda gazed at me with eyes that boiled over with envy. Then all of a sudden she put on a glassy look, like people do when their brains begin to work.

'I say!' she said suddenly. 'Why shouldn't you go to these Locketts instead of me?'

'Oh, but I couldn't,' I said.

'Why not?'

'Because – well, they're your friends, it's you they want.'

'But it isn't,' said Amanda. 'They only want Plum for their potty team, and somebody to ride her. They don't even know me, they've never seen me. Actually they'd much rather have you because you *can* ride, and you're keen, which is more than I am.'

'But you can't just –' I began feebly.

'You said your mother was away, and you're not doing anything. Why, Jill, it's a super idea.' Amanda began to brighten up. 'You take Plum and go to these Locketts tomorrow instead of me. You'll adore it.'

I shook my head dumbly.

'Oh, go on,' said Amanda. 'Don't be such a square.'

'Look here,' I said, rather crossly, 'I can't just go and dump myself on these people and say, you'll have to have me instead of Amanda. They might be livid.'

'Oh, if that's all,' Amanda said, 'I can ring them up now and ask them if it's all right.'

'I'd have to ring Mummy up tonight,' I said, 'and ask *her* if it's all right.'

The truth was, I had really fallen for the idea, and if I wasn't mistaken Amanda had actually suggested I could take Plum.

'Did you really mean,' I said, to get this cleared up, 'that you'd let me take your pony?'

'Of course,' said Amanda. 'It would stop her neighing with boredom quicker than anything.'

'All right,' I said. 'You can ring the Locketts, and if they say OK I'll ring Mummy. I might catch her now at her hotel, and if she says I can go, I'll go.'

'Wait here,' said Amanda, springing up and rushing out of the room. I really did feel as if I was dreaming now. The prospect of having a lot of fun and riding a pony like Plum with some horsy people was the sort of thing that doesn't happen to people very often, and I couldn't believe it was happening to me.

About five minutes later Amanda came back.

'It's OK,' she said. 'They said they'd love to have you, and you're to go tomorrow, and there's a horse box coming to fetch Plum and you can ride with the driver, like I was going to, and the Locketts will meet you at a crossroads near where they live. It's only thirty miles away.'

I felt stunned.

'I'd better go home and ring Mummy,' I said.

'Oh no, ring her from here,' said Amanda. 'I want this fixed, then I can breathe again.'

She took me down the hall to a library where the phone was. I rang Mummy's hotel in London, and she was in. I poured out the whole story, not very hopefully, expecting – to tell the truth – that I would get a flat no. But to my surprise Mummy said, 'That's rather nice, Jill. I know of the Locketts, in fact they're friends of some friends of mine, and they're awfully nice people, and if they really want you instead of Amanda, you go and enjoy yourself. Now do see that you take clean things, and pack properly, and behave well, and don't be silly, and do change whenever your feet are wet, and ask Miss Webb if she minds, and –'

'Oh, I will!' I said. 'Thanks awfully, Mummy. I'll see that everything's all right, and there go the pips again, goodbye!'

I was gasping for breath.

'Mummy says I can go,' I said to Amanda.

She smiled from ear to ear.

'Right! You be here at nine o'clock tomorrow.'

I went tearing home. Isn't it funny how adventures always crop up when you least expect them? I got my suitcase out from under my bed and started packing furiously. I kept out my best jodhs and jacket and a clean shirt to go in, and packed my black coat, and two more shirts – one was a bit scruffy, but reasonably clean – and I also shoved in my blue dress with the white squiggles, and my best shoes, and some odds and ends, and I even remembered handkerchiefs, and I opened my money box which had thirteen pounds in it which I had been saving up for something, but in the excitement of the moment I couldn't remember what. My yellow pullover that I would need was dirty, so I flew down to the kitchen and washed it and hung it out, hoping it would be dry by morning and if it wasn't it would be by the time I got to where I was going.

I expect by now you will be wondering what I was going to do about Black Boy and Rapide, my two ponies. I wasn't worrying about them at all. I knew that Mrs Darcy would be very glad to have them at the riding school, seeing it was August and people were taking a lot of extra lessons. I rang her up, and she said she would send Pansy round to fetch them.

Pansy arrived, and said, 'What's cooking, anyway?'

'Plenty,' I said. 'I'm going to stay with some people in the country, and do nothing but ride, and Amanda Applewood has lent me her perfect pony.'

Pansy gave a whistle.

'Go on? I didn't know you and Amanda were so thick.'

'Oh, it's a long story,' I said, 'but it's true.'

When Grace Webb arrived she didn't mind a bit about me going away, in fact I don't think she even grasped it, she was so wrapped up in some rather hideous, very artistic prints she had just bought at an antique shop. Before I went to bed that night I had told all my friends about my wonderful invitation and they said they envied me.

2 The invitation that wasn't

You know how it is when you are excited about something that is going to happen tomorrow? Next morning I woke up, thinking it was time to get up Hoo-jolly-ray, and looked at my watch, and it was only half-past five. I turned over and jammed my face down into the pillow, but I couldn't go to sleep again, so I thought I'd read. I hauled *The Horse in Sickness and in Health*, that fascinating classic, down from its shelf above my bed, but even that failed to grip and I only found myself reading the same three lines over and over again; so I gave up and began to imagine what the hospitable Locketts would be like.

I pictured Mr Lockett in immaculate riding clothes, with beautiful shining boots and a hacking jacket like Captain Cholly-Sawcutt's with leather patches on the elbows. Mrs Lockett would be vague and kind and unfussy, and keep on saying, 'Just do whatever you like, dear.' Then there would be two girls, one a year older and one a year younger than I, and just my sort of people; and a boy younger still so that he wouldn't boss us and think he knew everything – or should I make him older, about eighteen, and a cup winner at Richmond Horse Show, so that he'd be able to give us a lot of frightfully good coaching? I couldn't quite decide, but I knew that Fate would. I even gave the Lockett family an aged retainer who cooked divinely, and never thought of saying, 'You've had quite enough,' and would let us mess up her pans with sausages and chips whenever we wanted to. I found it quite easy to believe in this family I'd created, and it was so entrancing that before I knew it my watch said seven o'clock and I flew out of bed and dressed.

When the milkman arrived, he offered to take my suitcase up to Amanda's house; and feeling on top of the world and kindly disposed to everybody I made tea and took a cup up to Grace Webb, and reminded her for the umpteenth time about feeding the cats, the dog and the hens.

'And if you do forget anything,' I added, 'Mrs Crosby will remind you, and don't let her turn out my bedroom whatever she says, because she always puts my stuff away tidily, and if it's tidy I can't find it.'

After breakfast, although it was still too early, I set off and got to Amanda's house at half-past eight. The horse van and the driver were there already, and Plum, looking gorgeous with every hair shining, was being backed in. She looked at me as if to say, 'Who on earth are you?' and I could hardly believe that I was actually going to ride her.

'If you're the young lady that's going,' said the driver, 'you might as well get up in front. Your luggage is inside, and all the tack you'll need.'

'Where's Amanda?' I said, looking wildly round.

Just then the man in the white jacket who had provided us with yesterday's immense tea, came out of the house and said, just like they do in films, 'Miss Amanda's compliments, and she says she can't be bothered to get up, so you're to go on, and she hopes you'll enjoy yourself.'

I was thinking by now that Amanda was nothing if not cool, but I didn't care, it was all such fun, and

I jumped up into the seat next to the driver, and in five minutes we were off.

He proved to be one of those non-conversational people who never say anything but 'Ah!' and after I had said it was a lovely day, and he had said 'Ah,' and I had said, did he drive a lot of horses about in horse vans, and he had said 'Ah,' and I had said, was he keen on horses, and he had said 'Ah,' I gave up. We travelled slowly so as not to upset Plum, and did the run in an hour and a half. As we approached a crossroads, the driver broke his rule of only saying 'Ah,' and said, 'This'll be it.'

I looked out eagerly, because I was so sure that all the Locketts would be standing in a row to greet me, or at least Mr Lockett and the two girls and the younger (or older) boy. But the only person standing at the crossroads was a man in grey flannel slacks and a blue sweater, beside a small car.

My driver stopped, and the man came up to us.

'I'm called Lockett,' he said, 'and you must be the girl I've come to meet. We've only about a mile to go, so I suggest you get in the car with me, and the horse box can follow.'

'OK,' I said, and scrambled out, and got into the car.

I was feeling a bit odd, because when you have built up a dream and it starts working out wrong, you don't know where you are or how much more wrong it will go. I had been so sure about the two girls and the boy, and if I had had a horsy person coming to stay with me I should certainly have been there to meet her.

'Had a good journey?' said Mr Lockett as we moved off. He certainly seemed very kind.

I said I had, and he said, 'I hope the Wonder Pony has stood the trip well. She's got a great reputation.'

I just said Um, because I was a bit at sea.

'It's very nice of you to come,' went on Mr Lockett. 'Of course the whole idea is this One-Day Event is for teams. That is to say, there are no individual credits, you just win points for your team of six people, and we are only five, my three and their two cousins, so you'll be the sixth.'

'Oh,' I said politely.

'We had a sixth,' said Mr Lockett, 'but unfortunately she's broken her leg.'

'Oh,' I said again, beginning to feel uncomfortable, because I realised by now that I was a Double Substitute, that is, not only a substitute for Amanda but also a substitute for the one who had broken her leg, and it isn't always fun to be a substitute, much less a double one. My original wild excitement had dropped a couple of points.

'The others are at home,' said Mr Lockett. 'They would have come to meet you, but – er – they were rather busy.'

Now this was the last straw. I knew exactly what he meant, because I am psychic that way. I could picture the soul-chilling scene at the Locketts' home.

Mr Lockett: 'Now who's coming with me to meet this girl?'

Deathly hush.

Mr Lockett: 'Come on. Somebody's got to go and meet her.'

Deathly hush.

Mr Lockett: 'Well, make up your minds.'

Voices: 'Oh, Daddy, do we have to?'

'I promised I'd help Mummy.'

'I've got to go down to the saddler's.'

'You go!'

'No, I'm not going, you go.'

'I don't see why I should have to go.'

Mr Lockett: 'All right, I'll go by myself, but I think one of you might have made the effort.'

In other words, I was UNWELCOME, in large capital letters. For some obscure reason, nobody wanted me at the Locketts'. I couldn't understand it, but it was awful. I felt as if I had had a big bucket of cold water poured over me.

It looked to me as if there was some dark and sinister plot going on, and while dark and sinister plots are fine in thrillers they are not so hot when you yourself happen to be the victim.

'Oh,' I said, dimly.

Nothing else was said, and at last we got to the Locketts' house which was a large Victorian-type villa with two gables and a garden, standing all by itself in acres of scenery. Actually I wasn't in a mood to notice much.

Mr Lockett waited for the horse box to come up behind, and said to the driver, 'Go round to the back, I'll be with you in a minute.' Then he said to me, 'Come on in. I'll see to your pony while you freshen up.'

There didn't seem to be anybody about.

Mr Lockett said, rather uncomfortably, 'Where is everybody?' and then showed me into a dining-room and said, 'Wait here a minute.'

He left me and closed the door. I felt more awful still.

The window was wide open, and all I could see was a tangly garden and a lot of sky. The dining-room was very clean and chilly and empty, and what with the clock ticking and my heart thumping there seemed to be a lot of noise going on.

I waited a few minutes, and then suddenly I heard voices outside, quite near to the window.

Somebody said, 'She's come, and Daddy says she's dim and never says anything but "Oh".'

'That sounds harmless,' said another voice, 'and they say the pony's a wonder, and always wins, so that'll get us a lot of points which is all that matters.'

'Yes, but we've got to put up with *her*, and they say she's awful.'

I went cold all over, and then another voice broke in, 'Shut up, you dopes. The dining-room window's open and she can probably hear you.'

The first voice said, 'I don't care if she can, she's been wished on us anyway.'

I was furious by now, but more was to follow.

Apparently somebody else had joined the group outside, and was greeted with, 'Hello, Tom, Amanda's come.'

'Amanda? Oh, bad luck.'

Amanda? I thought. Amanda!

Then I saw it all. I had been tricked. That horrible Amanda had actually lied to me. She had never telephoned the Locketts at all, and they thought they had got Amanda and knew nothing about me. I wasn't cold now, I was boiling with rage and disappointment and humiliation. I was going to get out of this!

I made for the door, but before I could reach it, it opened and in came a very thin, grim-looking woman with a tray.

'Thought you might like a snack while you're waiting for your lunch,' she said, and slapped it down on the table and went out.

This rather took the wind out of my sails, so to speak. On the tray was a big cup of cocoa, two buttered scones which looked appetising, and a chocolate biscuit. I was terribly hungry because, truth to tell, I had been too excited to eat anything but a few cornflakes at breakfast.

I stood by the table, and found myself nibbling a scone while I tried to think. My impulse was to rush out of the room, tell these Locketts what I thought of them, and demand to be taken home at once.

But what if I did? How was I going to explain to all my friends whom I had told about my wonderful 'invitation'? I should look such a fool and I'd never live it down. And what would Mummy say? She would certainly say that I wasn't fit to be left at home alone when I could be so easily taken in.

Gloomily I sipped the cocoa, and as I did so someone came in who must, I guessed, be Mrs Lockett. She was neither vague nor in any other way as I'd imagined her, but was brisk and beaky and breezy and wearing very good riding clothes.

'Hello,' she said. 'Finished your snack? Well, hurry up and eat the rest, and I'll show you your room, and when you've unpacked you can show us your famous pony.'

Rather uncomfortably I said I didn't want any more, and she said, 'No appetite, eh?' and led me upstairs. At the top of the stairs she opened a door and showed me into a nice little room with a bed and a chair and chest of drawers, and on the wall a painting of two rather smudgy ponies in a paddock.

'Here you are,' she said, 'and there's your suitcase, so unpack at once. The girls' room is next door, and the bathroom's opposite. Come down as soon as you're ready.'

When she had gone I looked out of the window, still not knowing quite what to do. I hated the thought of staying, and yet I simply couldn't go home and confess that I'd been completely taken in by that beastly Amanda Applewood. Below me was a big stable yard, and a boy was leading Plum up and down. Plum looked beautiful, and looking at her my mouth fairly watered at the thought of riding her.

Right! I thought. I jolly well will. If they want me to be Amanda then I'll be Amanda. It isn't for long, I can stick it out, and as they expect Amanda to be awful, then I'll be awful. I'll be as awful as I can, and get all the fun that's going.

Hastily I opened my case and rammed the things into drawers; then I washed, brushed my hair, straightened my shirt and went downstairs.

3 A chilly welcome

They were all lined up.

'This is my lot,' said Mr Lockett. 'Phil, Mary and Jane. And these are the cousins – Tom and Lolly.'

Ten cold eyes stared at me blankly, and I stared back. These people all looked much of an age to me, except Lolly who was only about ten.

'Cheers!' I said ironically.

The eyes all blinked, and somebody said feebly, 'Hello, Amanda.'

'Do they call you Mandy at home?' said Mrs Lockett.

'No, they don't,' I said – with perfect truth!

'Then we'll just have to call you Amanda.'

'Gosh, what a mouthful!' said one of the girls.

'Oh, just call me Jill,' I said. 'That's what they call me at home.'

'Well, that does come easier, doesn't it?' said Mrs Lockett, and I could nearly see her mind working, thinking, 'If they wanted to call her Jill instead of Amanda, why didn't they call her Jill in the first place?'

'Well, come along, Amanda-I-mean-Jill,' said Mr Lockett, 'there's your pony, and we're dying to see her in action, so just take her round the paddock while we watch.'

At that moment I knew exactly how a goldfish feels in a bowl. All those eyes! And I had never touched

Plum in my life. I took the bridle and Plum gave me a Who-on-earth-are-you look which I hoped that nobody else noticed.

I led her firmly and nonchalantly towards the paddock, and she seemed docile enough; I suppose she was too overcome by all her experiences to be happy. I got up quickly and shortened the reins, holding her well in hand. She was extremely well schooled, and did a neat walk for me, then a reasonable trot and a rather reluctant canter. We made the circle of the not very large field, and came back to the others.

I got down.

'She's got a very pretty action,' said Mrs Lockett, 'but not much go, has she?'

'She's probably a bit seasick from the horse box,' I said, feeling I wanted to stick up for Plum. 'Anyway, she has enough go to have won about three thousand firsts, I know for a fact.'

As soon as I had made this stupid and unguarded remark, gross exaggeration and all, I knew I should have to be careful what I said.

'Well, you ought to know. You rode her,' said the oldest Lockett boy, and one of the girls muttered, 'Show-off!'

'Bags I have a try on her,' said the youngest girl, Lolly, and in one minute she was up on Plum, sitting almost on her neck like a jockey, and careering madly round the paddock. Plum had fairly come awake. You should have seen her! Throwing her head about, bucking like mad, tail streaming, eyes rolling – I can only say I was jolly glad she hadn't tried that on me.

'Crumbs!' said the Jane girl. 'Does she often behave like that?'

'You ought to know,' I said coldly. 'She's your cousin.'

'I meant the pony,' said Jane.

'If you meant the pony,' I said, determined to be as awful as Amanda was supposed to be, 'she naturally likes to be ridden by people with some idea of how to ride, not kids like monkeys.'

All the Locketts gave a gasp, and I felt myself giggling inside me.

'Lolly is the best rider of her age in the district,' said Mrs Lockett. 'Otherwise she wouldn't be in our team. And you get extra marks for a member of your team who's only ten.'

'You'll need them,' I said, being Awful Amanda again.

I could feel Jane, Mary, Phil, and Tom looking at me with loathing.

'Well, come along, children,' said Mrs Lockett, even more briskly than usual, 'there's just time for a little schooling before lunch. And we all know that Amanda – I mean Jill – is a terribly good rider with about three thousand rosettes, otherwise *she* wouldn't be in our team either.'

'Oh, if there's any winning to do, I'm the one,' I said airily, again giggling to myself at the looks of disgust that went round. I decided that before long I must get Plum away by myself and find out all about her.

The others fetched their ponies, a very nice lot; and with Mrs Lockett standing in the middle of the paddock and giving the commands, we all walked a circle, trotted, cantered, reversed, pulled up, and backed. I was keeping Plum on a very tight rein, and got told off for this, but I daren't be too free with her, not knowing her habits or she mine.

'I should have expected you to be a more relaxed rider,' said Mrs Lockett to me, as I drew level with her. 'Are you like this in the show ring?'

'Naturally,' I said haughtily, 'I can relax in the show ring because I know the sort of people I'm riding with. But as for *these* people, I haven't a clue what they'll do, and Plum loathes being crowded.'

Everybody looked at me in horror, and I thought, Well, I can't make myself much more unpopular, can I?

Actually by now I was feeling a bit guilty, but the thought of Amanda's treachery egged me on. I was jolly well going to give her a reputation that would take a lot of living down, and the fact that she had actually lied to me made me boil. I was getting more confident too, because Plum was really a lovely ride. At 14.2 she just suited me, her pace was smooth, and I felt that she could be made to do anything for me.

'Well, come along in now, kids,' said Mrs Lockett. 'It's only ten minutes till lunch.'

We all dismounted, and I said airily, 'What's the idea of this team thing, anyway?'

'It's a Show and Gymkhana,' said Mary, 'and everybody has to enter in teams of six. Nobody scores individual wins or prizes, but every win gets points for your side, and as there are only five of us we had to have another, as naturally we want to do well.'

'Oh, I see,' I said coolly. 'You want me to win everything so that you'll get some points.'

'Gosh, I say, I can't stand much more of this!' said Phil, going dark red and nearly spluttering. 'Who do you think you are? And what do you think *we* are — beginners?'

'I wouldn't know,' I said. 'But at first glance I would say that some of you need to learn to back without sawing your ponies' heads off, and all your stirrups are too short, and your hands are as stiff as clothes pegs, and as for your leg aids, they're just pretty crude.'

(All this, of course, was a libel.)

You should have heard the gasp that went round, and yet nobody spoke. I suppose they were struck dumb by my rudeness, and at the same time were trying to be polite to the guest, but I knew they were saving it up for me.

'Well, there's nothing like being candid,' said Mrs Lockett, giving me a loathing glance, 'but I suggest that in future you leave me to criticise the riding. I'm quite capable of it, I assure you, Amanda.'

'Jill,' I said sulkily.

'I suggest,' said Mrs Lockett briskly, 'that you others leave your ponies out here, and Jill can put hers into a loose box, as she's strange to the others and we don't know how they'll react.'

'Oh, I'd much rather,' I said loudly. 'I'm not keen on Plum mixing with ordinary ponies.'

That's done it! I thought, as I followed a stiff-backed Mrs Lockett towards the stable yard. It really was a very nice one, and had an archway and a clock, which I have always thought the height of richness. There were divided doors, now open, for the children's ponies, and two beautiful loose boxes.

'This one is for Plum,' said Mrs Lockett, showing me in. 'You'll be expected to keep it clean yourself. Phil and Tom got it ready for you before you came.' She gave me the sort of look that said plainly, 'And I don't think you deserve it, and if we'd known what you were like we wouldn't have had you at any price.'

It really was a lovely loose box and just the kind I would have liked to have at home, with a brick floor laid in a herring-bone pattern, and tiles halfway up the walls; and the manger was made of polished light wood, and full of fresh hay, and there was a rack for Plum's grooming tools which were standing in their box below waiting for me to unpack them.

I nearly said, 'Oh, it's gorgeous, thank you very much,' and then decided that Amanda probably wouldn't be as grateful as all that, so I said nothing, but began to unsaddle Plum.

When I was ready I went in to lunch, and we took our places at the dining-room table. In spite of the snack I had eaten, I was hungry. Everybody talked about people and things I hadn't heard of, and I didn't say a word, and they all avoided talking to me.

The lunch consisted, unfortunately, of all my *Un-*favourite foods: Scotch broth, a huge piece of boiled beef with carrots and potatoes, and baked apples and custard to follow. When it got to the baked apples I went all Amanda-ish and said 'No, thank you.'

'Don't you care for baked apples?' said Mrs Lockett, very hospitably. 'Is there anything you'd prefer?'

'What I like is fruit salad and ice cream,' I said, gloomily.

Everybody glared at me, and the little one, Lolly, said, 'You only get that at parties, not ordinary lunch.'

'It doesn't matter,' I said in a martyred voice. 'I'll do without.'

Just then the doorbell rang, and Phil said, 'That's the postman.' He went out, and came back with some letters, handing me one. It was registered. I thought it must be from Mummy, to whom of course I had given my address, so I tore it open and out fell a twenty pound note. I began to read the letter before I noticed that it began, 'My dear Amanda.' I had already taken in the first sentence, which said, 'I expect you will need some money, and I think you ought to treat the Locketts to ices and so on.'

'I'll have to answer this,' I said. 'Can I have some writing paper?'

'It's in that drawer,' said Phil. 'Get it yourself.'

'That's not very polite, Phil,' said Mr Lockett. 'Get the paper for Amanda.'

'She isn't very polite herself,' said Phil, obeying his father with a bad grace. 'Here you are,' he went on, practically chucking the paper and an envelope at me.

I went up to my room. The letter and money were from Amanda's mother, so of course I would have to send them to Amanda.

I wrote on the paper, 'Dear Amanda, this is for you, *Jill*,' and stuck it with Mrs Applewood's letter and the twenty pound note into the envelope and addressed it to Amanda's home. Then I went down again, and asked Mrs Lockett where the post was.

'You'll have to go to the village,' she said. 'It's about a mile. Look, Tom is going down. He can take it.'

I was just going to say thank you, and hand the letter over, when I realised that the letter was addressed to Miss Amanda Applewood! What would Tom think of me addressing a letter to myself? I really was just on the verge of giving the show away, and realised I would have to be careful; so I said I'd prefer to go myself, and Mrs Lockett looked at me as if I were a perfect pest, and said, 'Just as you like. Straight down the road, you can't miss it.'

I quite enjoyed the walk. It was a lovely day, and the road was a country lane with trees nearly meeting overhead, and hedges full of wild flowers. I wished I were cantering along the grass verge on my own pony, instead of living this difficult double life, and I had doubts about how I was going to keep it up. Having started being awful, I would have to keep on being awful, but it was a strain on my naturally beautiful disposition. Perhaps I could begin to slacken up on the rudeness by degrees, and let the Locketts think they were having a good influence on me; though actually I didn't know yet whether I was going to like the Locketts. I certainly hadn't given them a chance to show me what they were really like.

I found the post office and registered the letter. As well as being a post office it was also one of those village shops that sell everything, so I bought a Mars bar to make up for the baked apple that I hadn't had, and ate it thoughtfully as I walked back to Seaton Corner, which was the name of the Locketts' house.

I decided that as the countryside was so good, I would take Plum out for a ride by myself and get used to her.

When I got back to the house there didn't seem to be anybody about. I went into the dining-room, which was the only room I knew, and there was Mary sitting at the table mending her ankle socks.

'Oh, you're back,' said Mary. 'Well, just stay where you are, Amanda or Jill or whatever you call yourself, because I've got a few things to say to you. In the first place, we didn't want you here at all, we wanted Helen, the girl who's broken her leg; but we had to have somebody and Father and Mother know your parents, so they wrote and invited you to make up our team. I know you've got a perfect pony; but believe me, we could have done very well without you! There are other people as good, and a lot more pleasant. We know all about you, because we know a girl who goes to your school and she told us you were a horrible show-off. How right she was! She didn't tell us you were insulting, too, and disgustingly rude. Well, you are. So you can jolly well be decent, or you can jolly well go home, and if you do go home we'll jolly well see that your parents know why we can't stick you, and I don't suppose you'll want that. If you stay we'll be as polite to you as we can, but we shan't stand for any insults or any boasting about how marvellous you are. So you can make up your mind now, are you going or are you stopping?'

I thought furiously. Mary was quite right, I couldn't go home, only it wasn't for the reasons she thought. I wanted to stay, and I wanted to have fun, only I also wanted to go on being a bit Amanda-ish just to pay out Amanda. So I said, 'I want to stay,' in a rather sulky sort of way.

'Well, you heard what I said,' said Mary. 'Either join in and behave, or get out.'

'I thought of going for a ride by myself,' I said. 'Plum needs exercise.'

'That's all right by us,' said Mary.

I went out and saddled Plum, and rode her into the lane. Gradually all my troubles melted away, it was so lovely out there, and as we cantered along the grass verge I thought nothing could be better. When we came to an open common free from gorse or brambles I really tried Plum out to my heart's content. She was very well schooled, in fact a bit overschooled, I thought. I like a pony to have some independence and will of its own, otherwise you are not really riding it. With the lightest of aids Plum was cantering figures of eight and doing beautiful half-passes.

A man and boy stopped to watch, and the man said, with the camaraderie which you will have noticed belongs to horsy people, 'That's a nice pony you've got there. Practising for the show?'

'Um,' I said.

'Whose team are you in?'

'The Locketts,' I said without enthusiasm.

'And a nicer set of young people you wouldn't wish to find,' said the man – to which I didn't have to say anything, as he nodded and went off.

I practised everything I could think of with Plum, and she was so good it got nearly boring; then seeing it was past four o'clock I turned back towards the chilly welcome, so to speak, of Seaton Corner.

4   All those Locketts

I rode into the stable yard, and put Plum in her loose
box. I unsaddled her and rubbed her down, and I
must say Amanda had provided me with a super set
of grooming tools. There was even a halter made out
of scarlet webbing, with PLUM in gold letters across
the browband. I certainly never would have the nerve
to use that!

'Well, there you are, Plum,' I said; and looking at
me far from kindly through her long, long lashes,
Plum turned her head and gave me an unfriendly nip
on my forearm.

Oh dear, she doesn't like me either, I thought.

There was nobody about except for the small girl,
Lolly, who was practising low jumps in the paddock,
with a pole over two stools. I wandered into the house,
but it was horribly hushed and deserted. I would have
loved a cup of tea, or milk or lemonade, but there was
nobody to suggest it, and I thought longingly of how
at home I would have rushed into the kitchen and got
it myself. I really began to feel very homesick and
neglected, and realised it was my own fault for going
on being Amanda. It was a lesson to me for life, never
to be really beastly or mean and get myself hated.

I wandered out into the yard again, and leaned
on the gate watching Lolly. She seemed a very
persevering kid, going on and on at her little jump
and taking no notice of me. She wasn't a bad-looking

kid and she sat her pony very well; he was a small Welsh pony, not more than 12 hands and very nicely built, with a narrow intelligent head.

I noticed her idea was to give him the Hup! at the right split second, and not leave it to him, which I thought was quite enterprising for a kid of nine or ten.

I thought she hadn't noticed me at all, but after a few minutes she gave me a rather cross look, and said, 'I wish you'd clear out. You're putting me off.'

'Sorry,' I said, forgetting for the moment to be Amanda. 'I thought you were doing very well.'

She looked surprised.

'Oh, do you really? I've got to practise a lot, and I like doing it when the others are out because they all try and teach me at once, and then I go and muck it up, and no wonder.'

'You're pretty young,' I said, 'to be in the team' – and then I thought she'd probably take offence at that, because nobody likes to be told they're pretty young. But she didn't seem to mind.

'Well, that's the idea,' she said. 'You see, at the show they'll give points for every win. I think it's six points for a first, four for a second, two for a third, and one for a fourth – when there is a fourth. Well, if you happen to be under twelve and win for your team, you get bonus points. I mean, if I should win the under-fourteen jumping – which isn't very likely – I'd get about six bonus points and that would be quite something, wouldn't it?'

'How high can your pony jump?' I asked. 'You're only on about two-foot now.'

'Oh yes, but that's only for practising take-off, like I'm doing. I think you impress the judges if you do a proper take-off, and don't just leave it to the pony, like a lot of kids do. Actually Gelert can do three-foot jumps easily. In fact I once got third place in an under-fourteen jumping, and most of the kids were thirteenish. I mean, I'm not bragging or anything, I'm just telling you.'

'Jolly good,' I said. 'But Gelert's a dog's name, isn't it?'

'Was,' said Lolly, tightening her reins. 'But now it's a pony's name. Do you think I should stick some brushwood along this jump, and do it again?'

'Where is there some?' I said.

'Over there, in the ditch.'

'I'll get it,' I said, and went and fetched a huge armful and arranged it along the jump where it bristled up about another six inches.

'Thanks very much,' said Lolly. 'Now stand clear.'

But Gelert didn't like the look of the brushwood and he muffed the jump, ignoring Lolly's aids.

'I mucked that,' she said in disgust.

'No, you didn't,' I assured her. 'You gave the right aids, but Gelert wasn't having any. You'll have to keep him to it, don't let him get away with it.'

'OK,' she said. 'Here goes.'

This time she did a very nice, neat jump. I told her that if I were her I should leave it at that, as the pony had had enough, and it was always the right thing to finish up on a good achievement.

'I say,' she said, 'you're not so bad really. Only you've jolly well put the others' eyes out with all your bragging. You'd better look out. They're gunning for you, and they've decided that they're not going to speak to you at all unless you apologise, and even if you do, they don't think you're so hot.'

I bit my finger, and said, 'Well, I just say what I think.'

'Coo, you should have heard Phil and Mary going on about you,' said Lolly. 'They think you're the pits. Jane says she doesn't care what sort of person you are so long as you can win things; and my brother Tom's the sort of person that rude remarks roll off, if you know what I mean. Not that he likes you, of course.'

She came in, and I helped her to unsaddle Gelert and rub him down; then she turned him into the field.

'Ours stay out,' she said. 'It's only your wonder-pony that gets a loose box.'

I nearly said, 'Well, I'd better look after her, seeing she isn't mine,' but fortunately caught myself in time! The perils of living a double life are always with you, to trip you up.

I was so grateful to have some human company that I stuck with Lolly, and in the end she took me upstairs and showed me her pony album, which was a big scrapbook full of pictures she'd cut out of papers and magazines, all ponies and horses. She had hundreds. I told her about my pony frieze round my bedroom at home, and she said she thought it was a smashing idea and she'd love to see it. Of course I'd been describing my own home, not Amanda's palatial residence, and again I thought I'd have to be careful.

Suddenly the door opened and in came Mary and Jane. They looked very surprised to see me there with Lolly, and Mary said icily, 'Your room's next door. This is our room.'

I nearly explained, and said I was sorry; but I decided I'd better be a bit Amanda-ish, so I said, 'You can have it. I don't want it.'

'Oh, we were having quite a nice time,' said Lolly.

I went into my room and sat on the bed. I was frightfully hungry, and wished it was teatime. In the end I washed, and took off my jodhpurs and put on my school skirt, and brushed my hair, and at last the tea bell rang. I felt I didn't care what there was for tea, not even if it was sardines which are my most Sordid Tea, but it turned out to be buttered eggs, which was gorgeous.

'I hope there's something you like,' said Mrs Lockett a bit sarkily.

'Oh yes, thank you, it's super,' I said.

Everybody looked stunned and I ate madly, mopping up piles of bread and butter, till Tom said, 'Hold on, some of us want a bit too.'

I felt myself going scarlet, and mumbled, 'Sorry.'

'Gosh!' said Jane. 'She said "sorry". You wouldn't have thought she knew such a word.'

'Now that's enough, Jane,' said Mr Lockett. 'What have you been doing all afternoon, Amanda?'

'I'd rather you called me Jill,' I said, 'and I've had quite a nice afternoon. I went to the village, and then I took Plum out for some exercise, and then I watched Lolly jumping.'

'She thought I was good,' said Lolly.

'Very gracious of her,' said Phil, glowering at me.

'She is good,' I said, 'and she works hard.'

Again they all looked stunned, so I thought I'd better shove in a bit of Amanda, and added, 'Of course, I don't mean "good" in the same class that I'm good myself.'

'Blimey!' said Tom. 'She's past hope. We'll just have to put up with her. Hogging all the bread and butter, and everything.'

After tea the girls started clearing the table, and I stood about awkwardly, wondering what to do next and hoping they would suggest something;

but somehow everybody melted away and I found myself alone.

I sat on a chair in the dining-room, but nobody came.

When I got sick of this, I went up to my room and read *Precious Bane*, which I had brought with me because I was halfway through it, but I couldn't help thinking what a lovely evening it was and how much I should like to have been with the others, doing whatever they were doing. Again I felt homesick, and thought once more, This ought to teach people not to be nasty. It's so rotten not to be wanted.

At half-past eight there was a bang on my door, and in came Lolly.

'Are you coming down for cocoa?' she said. 'Or I'll bring it up here, if you like. Mary said it wouldn't be a bad idea.'

'Oh, all right,' I said, with a sinking heart, realising that they didn't want to see any more of me tonight.

Lolly brought up a beaker of cocoa and a fat slice of homemade cake.

'I'm going to bed now,' she said. 'Everybody goes to bed at nine, so you're not missing much. And if I were you, I'd jolly well say I was sorry tomorrow, because you can't be enjoying yourself.'

I drank my solitary cocoa, and I knew just what the Prisoner of Chillon and all that lot felt like.

Next morning there was a bang on my door at half-past seven, and I jumped out of bed, threw on my dressing-gown and went to the bathroom; rushed in and had a bath. When I came out there were a lot of people standing outside, looking very glum.

'There are turns for the bathroom,' said Jane, 'and it wasn't yours.'

'Oh yes, it was,' I said. 'I'm the guest and guests

always go first. Anyway, I must say the water wasn't very hot. It's always boiling at home.'

'Pity you didn't stay there,' said Mary.

I dressed in my blue shirt and jodhpurs, and when the breakfast bell rang at eight o'clock I strolled down. You will think we never did anything but have meals at Seaton Corner, but actually I am describing them because it seemed to be the only time I ever had any human company.

'We're all going for a ride this morning,' said Mrs Lockett.

'Good,' I said. 'By the way, do I get first bathroom, or don't I?'

Mrs Lockett looked a bit taken back.

'You do if you're quick,' she said. 'Not more than five minutes, though.'

'As long as everybody understands that,' I said.

The others all looked at me down their noses, and said nothing, but went on eating. When we had finished, Mrs Lockett said, 'Now hurry up and get everything cleared, and it's your turn to help Mrs Place, Jane and Lolly; and everybody else get your beds made and rooms tidied, and we'll be ready to start at ten.'

Mr Lockett wiped his mouth, and said, 'Look at the time, I'll have to rush.'

It turned out later that he was estate agent to somebody called Lord Crispwater.

I did my room, still feeling like the Prisoner of Chillon, and then wandered down to the yard to get Plum ready. Plum looked at me more amiably this morning, I suppose she was getting used to seeing me around, and I didn't feel she was all that devoted to Amanda Applewood, anyway.

After a while the others came trickling out of the

house, and began to catch their ponies in the field. Jane was grumbling that she had shelled about ten pounds of peas while Lolly had only dried the dishes.

Nobody took any notice of me until Mrs Lockett came out, also dressed for riding, and said, 'Are you ready, Jill? Come along, everybody.'

Mrs Lockett had a very nice chestnut mare. Phil and Mary had almost identical black ponies, except that Phil's had a white flash, and Mary's had four white socks. They were called Opal and Agate. Jane's pony was a frisky roan with black mane and tail, called Nice Weather, and Tom had a very high-spirited light chestnut called Commodore. They all looked keen, and we went clopping out into the lane and formed a neat string, with me meekly bringing up the rear. Mrs Lockett told us to do an extended walk, which we did, except that Nice Weather was given to bucking; then Lolly's pony, Gelert, hung back and came alongside me, which Plum seemed to resent and to my horror she suddenly threw her head up and charged fiercely to the front of the string.

'Jill had better learn to control that pony,' said Phil. 'Don't you think so, Mother?'

'Use your legs, use your legs!' muttered Mrs Lockett to me.

'I was,' I said. I couldn't explain that I wasn't sufficiently used to Plum to anticipate her.

'Well, everybody stop and we'll get organised again,' said Mrs Lockett, and everybody stopped, including Plum, so suddenly that she was a bit too quick in the uptake for me, and I bounced in the saddle and wobbled.

'You're sure you're all right, Jill?' said Mrs Lockett. 'You really must take things more steadily.'

I went scarlet, and was glad to collect Plum and

resume my place at the back where I went very cautiously indeed.

The summer sun came filtering pleasantly through the trees, and at the end of the lane we forked to the right across some sparse woodland with broad tracks where we were able to canter. The others went ahead, but I was a bit unsure of Plum so I held back until Mrs Lockett rose in her saddle, turned, and yelled to me, 'Come on, slowcoach!'

This annoyed me so much that I felt, 'Now I'll show you!' and I gave Plum her head, and off we flew. I got in front of the others, which was a bit silly seeing I didn't know the country, and in a moment I saw that the track ended with a five-barred gate. The sensible thing would have been to pull up and open the gate for the others, but I was so mad I didn't care, and Plum didn't seem to want to pull up, anyway. I really was fool-headed, because I had no idea of Plum's jumping capacity, but it was too late now to stop her, she went straight for the gate. I managed to collect her, and over we flew with inches to spare and landed – fortunately – in a soft, rutty lane. Then I pulled her up and waited.

The others dismounted and Tom opened the gate for them to go through.

'That wasn't very clever of you, Jill,' said Mrs Lockett dryly. 'If you want to show us how well Plum jumps, do it in the paddock at home, not in open country that you don't know, and over a five-foot gate. If you break your neck, I'll have the job of explaining to your mother, won't I? Just be a bit more considerate.'

I felt miserable, and made up my mind that for the rest of the ride I would be a perfect slug. We crawled along a rough farm road, and through a farmyard, and turned into a stubble field where the going was poor.

I didn't like it much because Plum kept stumbling – she was obviously a temperamental pony, and loathed poor going, like a ballerina who has to dance on a school platform all knots and bumps; but at last we got out of that and – hurray! – there was lovely parkland ahead of us, and Mrs Lockett opened a gate and led us in. It was simply wonderful across the park, and as the others streamed away, so did I. This just suited Plum; she was a gorgeous ride, so smooth that it was like flying. I could easily have passed the others while keeping her fully controlled, but I felt I mustn't do that, though it was a shame to have to check her at all. We all galloped for a distance, and then a brook lay ahead, and beyond it a meadow track. I hung back and let the others take the jump first, as I felt was expected of me. Plum fairly flew over, her jumping was obviously perfect. Then off we went again, and up a hill which slowed everybody down except Plum, and again I had to check her, which she didn't enjoy.

'We'll halt,' ordered Mrs Lockett. 'Everybody get down.'

We all stopped and dismounted, and Phil unfastened his saddle-bag and gave everybody an apple all round.

'Isn't it gorgeous?' said Jane. 'It's the best ride we've had for ages.'

'I'm doing pretty well,' said Lolly. 'I've kept up with you lot, anyway.'

'Sure you haven't had enough?' said Mrs Lockett. 'Would you like to go back, if Jane will go with you?'

Lolly said, not likely, and when we had had a breather we all remounted.

'Now remember,' said Mrs Lockett, 'at the top of the hill there's a short woodland track and then a gate.

We stop at the gate, and cross the main road, and into the woods on the other side, and down Brinkwell Valley.' We went off, and Phil, Mary and Tom got ahead while I hung back deliberately with Jane and Lolly. After we crossed a main road, we were in some beautiful woods where we had to meander around trees by a narrow track, and then we went bounding down a hill where Jane and Lolly both came to grief and got unseated. Instinctively I stopped to help them, which they seemed to find surprising. I suppose Amanda would just have charged on regardless, but it was hard to be Amanda all the time when I have naturally such a different disposition.

The others waited for us, and Mrs Lockett said, 'There's a sort of water jump in a minute, a low bank with a ditch on the other side. I thought I'd prepare you, so if any of you don't fancy it you can turn left and cross it on a culvert. It isn't really difficult.'

Of course nobody was going to funk the jump, so off we went until we saw it ahead, and then chose a place to take it. Mrs Lockett, Tom, and Mary went over simultaneously though well spaced, then Jane and Phil. I collected Plum, and as I did so heard Lolly say, 'Oh, I don't think I'll jump,' but I hadn't time to see what happened because I was already in the air. Believe me, to this day I don't know what Plum did. I only know that I saw the ground just before I slapped down on it, and Plum's hoofs missing my nut by inches, and there was a sort of swishing of the air as she whizzed by above me at full speed, and away she galloped with her reins trailing.

Talk about being mortified! I jumped up promptly as one is taught to do, and yelled 'Plum! Hoy! Whoa! Whoa, you beast!' Which was quite useless. By now the two boys were galloping after Plum, but what a hope. She was so much faster than their ponies, as I had already proved, and having been held in check for most of the morning was all for a gallop.

'Are you all right?' said Mrs Lockett. 'Good gracious, what happened?'

'Yes, I'm all right. I don't know,' I muttered, feeling very humiliated, and answering both questions in the same breath.

'Boys, boys, come back, it's useless!' Mrs Lockett shrieked, and added, 'They'll be breaking their necks at that uncontrolled speed. She'll have to look after herself, and if she wrecks herself I can't help it.'

The boys came back, and Phil said to me, 'You go at the jumps as if you were barmy. Your pony's out of sight.'

'All right,' I said. 'I'll go after her on foot, you lot go on home. She'll stop soon, I expect.' And I strode away furiously. Lolly, who had crossed the ditch by the culvert, came after me, and kindly said, 'I'll come with you.' I didn't look back to see what the others were doing – actually they were waiting, expecting me to turn back – but I went on, and soon in a dingle I came upon Plum, looking very sorry for herself. She had tried to jump a broken rail fence, and her reins had caught, and she was practically hanging. I went and released her. Her forelegs and shoulders were bleeding, and she looked a mess and was trembling; I was terrified she might be lamed, though she stood straight.

'Is she all right?' said Lolly.

'Seems to be,' I said curtly, leading Plum out.

'I expect she was a frightfully expensive pony, she looks it,' said Lolly.

'I wouldn't know,' I said, and realised that once more I had nearly given myself away, but Lolly was too young to twig. If it had been one of the others, they would have said, 'Fancy not knowing what your own pony is worth!'

'We'd better go back to the others,' said Lolly.

'You can, I'm not,' I said bitterly. 'I'll make my own way home, thank you.' It was a bit silly of me, but I was shaken by the fall and upset because I had seemed to have made a fool of myself at the jump (though it wasn't really my fault), and worried in case Plum was really hurt.

I led her, and scrambled out of the dingle, making for a gate that opened into a road and leaving Lolly standing, not knowing what to do. In the end I suppose she went back to the others, because I found myself alone on the road and didn't know which way to turn. I plumped for left as being most likely, and on we trudged, being overtaken by a lot of traffic. Every time a car passed, Plum threw her head and side-skipped, it was horrible. After a bit I met a man walking, and asked him the way back to Seaton Corner, and he told me I was going in the wrong direction, and if I turned round it would be straight on, second right, across the common, and in all about eight miles.

My heart was in my boots, but I reversed, and off we went again, the way we had come. To make things worse, a cold wind sprang up, and down came a nasty shower. I decided that Plum was fit to ride, and up I got, but she hated the metalled road which had no grass verge at all, so we went very slowly, and I had to steady her down every time we met traffic or were passed.

I bet she gets pneumonia! I thought dismally. She'll probably die, and that'll be the end of Plum, and the end of me too, as everybody will blame me, and why did I come to this gruesome place, anyway?

I tried to sing to myself as I had been told one should when finding oneself in the midst of a rather messy plight, but all I could think of was hideously sad songs like *Here a sheer bulk lies poor Tom Bowling* and *You got me crying, baby*. I felt as if I had been on the way for hours, and I was frightfully hungry. Just as I was wishing I was on the moon or the Channel Islands, or somewhere, anywhere but here, I saw a horse box coming towards me, and to my surprise it stopped.

Phil got down.

'Oh, there you are,' he said. 'Why on earth did you go off like that? You really are the maddest girl.'

The driver got down too, and they opened the back of the box and led Plum in. Then we all three got up on the front seat.

'When Lolly said you'd gone off on your own, I galloped home and got the horse box,' said Phil. 'Why didn't you wait, or come back? We expected you to.'

'Oh, did you?' I snapped. 'I was just fed up with being made a fool of.'

'Nobody was making a fool of you,' said Phil, 'only we were a bit surprised that you didn't seem to have much control over that wonder-pony of yours. She doesn't take much notice of you, does she?'

There just wasn't anything I could say, short of explaining that as Plum wasn't my pony at all I couldn't be expected to be used to her little ways, so I didn't say a word.

'You scared the living daylights out of Mum,' said Phil reproachfully.

At last we got back to the house. Mrs Lockett was quite fussy over me, and said, 'I've kept your dinner, but you must go up and have a hot bath first. The vet is coming to look at Plum, so don't worry about that. Are you sure you're not concussed or anything?'

I didn't feel a bit concussed, but I was tired and hungry and wet, and glad to get upstairs; and then up came Mrs Lockett herself with a hot cup of tea, and I couldn't help saying, 'I'm sorry I've made such a lot of trouble for you.'

She looked surprised, and said, 'Oh, that's all right, only it is a good thing not to be impetuous or go at everything blindly. Even if you have got a fine pony, you've got to ride her and not let her master you. And when you give your pony an order or an aid, and she doesn't obey you, you've got to keep right on until she does. Don't let her get away with it, and think it doesn't matter.'

This was awfully good sense, and I was longing to say, 'Yes, you're quite right, and if only I had my own Black Boy or Rapide here I'd show you I can control a pony.'

But I just muttered, 'Thank you very much, I'll try,' – and fled into the bathroom. I felt it was hopeless trying to go on being a beast to Mrs Lockett, because she really was kind and a thoroughly horsy person of the sort I could admire.

After I had finished my late lunch there was no sign of the others. The vet said that Plum was quite all right, only a bit upset so that she shouldn't be ridden again that day; so as the sun had come out, I went and sat on a seat in the garden and Mrs Lockett gave me some copies of *Horse and Hound* to read. I thought this would be rather nice, until I found I had read them all before.

5   All that schooling

The next morning I simply didn't get a chance at the bathroom until everybody else had done, they saw to that! Consequently I wasn't dressed when the breakfast bell rang, and I came down late, alone. As I walked down the stairs I heard a knock at the front door, and some letters came through the box and fell on the mat.

Of course I went to pick them up, like one does, and the very first one was addressed to me. I mean, really to me – 'Miss Jill Crewe'. Horrors! I thought. Supposing somebody else had picked it up! It was only the merest chance that it was me. I guessed it must be from Mummy, but then I saw that I didn't know the writing, though the postmark was Chatton. I put it in the pocket of my jodhs, and went into the dining-room where they were all sitting round the table.

'Did I hear the post?' said Mr Lockett. 'Were there any letters, Jill?'

'There was one for me,' I mumbled.

'Was that all?'

'Well, there were some others –' I began, going red, and Mary said, 'Do you mean to say you only brought your own letter? Gosh, how self-centred can people get!'

I kept my face down to my plate and went on mopping up my cornflakes, while Lolly went out to get the other letters. Directly breakfast was over I rushed up to my room and opened my letter. It was from Amanda Applewood.

It said:

Dear Jill,

I hope you are enjoying yourself, I expect you are, because you like loads of riding. I bet the Locketts' eyes popped when they saw you instead of me, and I hope you have forgiven me for pulling a fast one on you about the telephone call, because I couldn't risk them not wanting you and me having to go instead. But as Shakespeare says, all's well that ends well. I am having a lovely time, because I stop in bed reading comics all the morning and go to the pictures in the afternoon, which I couldn't do if Mummy was at home, and I watch the telly at night till it stops instead of getting shoved off to bed at nine when the best programme starts.

So mind you go and win everything on Plum! Jolly good luck!
Yours ever,
Amanda
P.S. Don't give Plum any sugar after she's groomed, as she grinds it up and dribbles it down her front.

When I had read this I was livid, and my first idea was to write Amanda a snorter and tell her what was happening, and that I was jolly well being her and making the Locketts hate me, and I hoped she'd enjoy living it down after I'd gone; and then I thought I'd better not in case she promptly wrote to the Locketts and spilled the beans and I had to go home in what is called Ignominy. So I decided that I would ignore the letter in a dignified way, and leave Amanda guessing.

I made my bed and tidied away my things which had a way of strewing themselves all over the place, and then I went down. Everybody was clustered round the dining-room table, trying to look at the same thing. Mary said, 'Oh, there you are. The schedule for the Show has come and we're deciding about the entries. Some of us will be entering for everything, of course. I suppose that's OK by your Royal Highness?'

'I'm not fussy,' I said, flopping on the settee. 'Stick me down for anything you like, sixteen and under.'

'What about the gymkhana events?' asked Phil. 'Is it beneath your precious Plum's dignity to do Musical Mats?'

'On the contrary,' I said, 'I'm pretty hot at Musical Mats.'

'I shouldn't be too hot,' said Mary. 'You were supposed to be jolly hot at country riding, and look where it got you yesterday.'

I felt squashed and uncomfortable.

'What about this Hunter Hurdle?' said Phil. 'It gets a lot of points. We think the whole team should enter for it. It's one of those up-hill-and-down-dale things – very tough.'

I said that suited me, but actually I was wondering what Plum would be like on such a course. I hadn't had a chance of finding out. She had taken a five-foot gate like a bird, and then toppled me off at a medium water jump.

'Am I in the Hunter Hurdle?' shouted Lolly, jumping up and down.

'You'll have to be,' said Jane, 'worse luck, because you're in the team. How you'll go on I hate to think. The jumps will be enormous, and you have to gallop downhill which you can't do, and there's a water jump and turn at the bottom always, and you'll get on the wrong leg and overbalance, and the whole thing's run to time. You've a hope!'

'All right, all right,' said Lolly, her eyes sparkling. 'So what? And I *can* do it, and it comes well from you, talking about getting on the wrong leg. Just you tell me, you jolly well tell everybody, who cantered a whole figure of eight on the wrong leg at Wickham Show? Go on – who did? Just tell me that.'

'Oh, shut up,' said Jane.

'Well, who did? It wasn't me! I wasn't on the wrong leg.'

'Shut up, Lolly,' said Tom.

'Well, Jane did,' said Lolly. 'And she didn't even know it till the judge flipping well told her.'

'You know you're not allowed to say flipping,' said Jane. 'Let's get on with the schedule. I want to do all the gymkhana events for the juniors. And the showing class, and the junior jumping. I've had two second places this season for jumping, so I might pull off something there.'

'I'm doing junior jumping too,' said Lolly. 'And I might beat you, Jane. And I get an age allowance too, if I win. So if we both get clear rounds and have to jump off, it would pay you to let me win.'

'I never heard such nerve!' said Phil. 'You really are the limit, Lolly, for a kid.'

'Oh, don't take any notice of her,' said Mary, 'or she'll argue all day. Tom isn't fifteen yet, so he can go in for both jumping events, and Phil and Jill and I will do the senior showing class and a lot of games, if we've the strength.'

'Where does the Hunter competition come into the schedule?' I asked. 'I hope it's pretty far from the senior jumping or the ponies will conk out.'

'It comes in the morning,' said Phil, 'and the senior jumping in the afternoon. That's the most important competition, actually. Without showing side, Mary and I have been beating each other all through this season, so if we manage to pull off first and second that'll be some lovely points for the team.'

'And where am I supposed to come in?' I said cheekily. 'Third? Or nowhere?'

'Look,' said Mary, sticking her elbows on the table, 'while we're on this subject let's have an understanding. If we're going to ride as a good team we'd better stop bickering. Everybody has got to do their best, and no more getting at each other. So do you think, Jill, that for the next week or so you could stop getting into people's hair? Just ride, that's all we ask of you. Because if you can't pipe down you'd better clear off home and have done with it.'

'In other words,' said Phil, 'we humbly acknowledge that we're hopeless compared with Your Highness, so shall we leave it at that? No more wisecracks?'

'Suits me,' I said, shrugging my shoulders.

'Hurray,' said Mary. 'Chuck over a piece of clean paper, Jane, this bit looks like a spider's web. Now I'll get it all written out and copied on the form, and Phil can do the adding up for the entry fees.'

She began to write with great concentration and we all kept quiet. It took ages to work out and copy on to the entry form, but at last it was completed.

'Now,' said Mary, 'I'll read it over and you can all check. I say, doesn't it look nice – The Locketts – here, where it says, "Name of Team". Isn't it solemn – we've really started something.'

'Let's hope we finish something,' said Phil, when Mary had finished reading. 'Now do you think you could all keep up this unnatural silence and peace while I try to do the accounts? I've got all those entry fees to work out and add up, and I can't do it in the middle of the usual family din.'

Everybody froze into a kind of trance and tried not to sneeze or anything.

Phil began to scribble on a piece of rough paper and to add up, and finally said, 'Well, being the only mathematician in the family, and self-appointed accountant, I make it twenty-six pounds seventy for the lot.'

'Are you sure you've got everything down?' said Mary.

'I think so. And it doesn't really matter, because one can always enter or scratch up to the time of the competition.'

'Twenty-six pounds seventy!' said Jane. 'What a fortune.'

'It's only four pounds something each,' said Mary, 'and if we don't win it back – and more – there'll be something wrong with our riding. The first prize is two hundred and fifty pounds, and the second is one hundred and seventy-five, and the third is one hundred. We've got to be in the first three'.

'Two hundred and fifty pounds!' said Jane, with her eyes like saucers. She counted madly on her fingers, and said, 'That's forty one pounds something each. I never had so much money in my life.'

'You haven't got it now,' said Tom dryly.

Jane said she had as good as got it, and if she and Mary joined they could buy a good camera between them, and plenty of films, and Phil said, 'That's right, spend it before you've even won it. You might at least think of buying something for the pony that won it for you. I shall spend mine on that absolutely smashing double bridle in Adams's window.'

'Who's spending what?' said Mrs Lockett, as she came in.

Tom explained, and I must say I rather sympathised with Jane, as I am just the same and always spend my prize before I win it, sometimes with disappointing results. On this occasion I couldn't help thinking how marvellous if our team really did win the first prize, or even any prize, and I had some money to take home.

'Some of us have entered for everything,' said Phil, 'and of course we're in all the team jobs. Everybody owes me four pounds forty-five, so dig out your hidden hoards, folks, and Mother can write the cheque. Now we're really in the competition.'

'And still sitting round the breakfast table!' Mrs Lockett pointed out. 'I'm ready to have a session with you people. From now on we've got to take this business seriously, so get your ponies ready and meet me in the paddock in thirty minutes.'

'Ready?' said Jane. 'We're ready now, aren't we?'

'What I meant,' said Mrs Lockett, 'was that I expect to see the ponies in show condition, perfectly groomed.'

'What! On an ordinary day?' said Tom.

'He just flicks Commodore over with a dirty stable rubber,' said Lolly, being an absolute traitor to her brother.

'That's enough, Lolly,' said Mrs Lockett. 'This morning we'll parade in full style. We're taking life seriously from now on.'

'Quite right,' said Phil. 'Proper grooming, everybody – and it may interest you to know that I've done Opal already – before breakfast.'

Everybody yelled, and Mary retorted, 'I helped to *get* breakfast!'

We all tumbled out into the yard in the crisp morning air, and got down to business. I found Plum in a cooperative mood. She loved being groomed, and it was easy to use such beautiful equipment as Amanda had provided me with. I washed and brushed and polished, taking very little notice of what was going on outside until a terrible din broke out.

Jane and Lolly were throwing soapy sponges and saddle soap at each other and having a free fight. Tom came along and tried to break it up, and Jane grabbed a bucket half full of water and threw it at him, and Tom dodged and the water went all over Lolly. This stopped everything.

'Now look what you've done,' said Lolly, furious. 'I'm soaked. I'll have to go in and change.'

'Well, it was your own fault,' said Jane. 'You started this fight, pinching my dandy brush.'

Suddenly Mrs Lockett appeared. 'I never saw anything like you children,' she said. 'You're the limit. Look at the state of this yard! There's no time now, so leave the mess as it is, and when we've finished you two can come back and collect all these rags and sponges and buckets, and sweep up the water; and if you miss the first course at lunch that'll be just too bad, because nobody's going to wait for you.'

Jane and Lolly looked suitably crushed, and fled to tidy themselves and finish off their ponies; and soon we all came out, with shining ponies, and made our way to the paddock.

'Gather round,' said Mrs Lockett, 'and we'll go into conference about our training which has to be taken seriously. What I propose first is schooling, schooling, and more schooling. I suggest we begin with a really hard morning on basic riding.'

'Mother,' said Mary, 'do we really need so much schooling? We're not exactly beginners. Honestly, we're as good as anybody in the Pony Club, and better than a lot of them.'

Phil and Tom said, 'That's right.'

'And are you contented to be as good as the others?' said Mrs Lockett. 'Are you? Because I'm not. There's quality in riding, and I want my crowd to have it, not only because it wins competitions but for its own sake. I know the standard in most showing classes is mediocre, but that doesn't give you the right to be satisfied with yourselves, or to say, "I'm a bit better than most of them, so I'm pretty sure to get placed." If any of you win a showing class I'd like to think it was on real merit, and the judges weren't saying, "Well, he or she is the best of a poor lot." '

'That's true,' said Phil. 'Well, let's get going with it. I'm ready to go back to the beginning and be shown. What do you want us to do?'

Mrs Lockett suggested that we should begin by mounting, and riding the circle at a walk so that she could see how we were sitting.

'Well, that's easy,' said Jane rashly. 'That won't kill us.'

Mary gave her a pitying look. 'That's what you think. You ought to know Mother's little sessions by now.'

Mrs Lockett said, 'Phil, will you lead, please.'

I was glad I hadn't been asked to lead, though I was sure I was sitting correctly and enjoying Plum's light and easy action. We walked round and round, round and round, and for a long time Mrs Lockett said nothing and I wondered if she intended to let

us go on till lunchtime. Of course her idea was that
though we might all start off well, before long some
people would slump and slacken off and show faults
in position.

This began to happen, and when Mrs Lockett at last
came to life she found plenty to say. She started with
Phil; every time he corrected his position, she said, he
jerked instead of flowed.

'I wasn't aware of it,' said Phil.

'Just remember the poetry of motion,' said Mrs
Lockett. 'Your movements should be almost imper-
ceptible. Now you, Jill.' I wondered what she was
going to say about me. 'Your pony has a beautiful
action, but really you're trading on that. You don't
look so beautiful yourself because you're stiff and
unyielding, you've got into the right position and
you're going to hold it if it kills you. You look like
something in the Royal Academy.'

I loosened up quickly, and was told, 'Now you look
as if you were on a swing. Just look easy and stay easy.
It's the staying that's the hard part. Anybody can look
right for a few minutes.'

Mary next came in for criticism. She had her legs
too far forward so that her heels weren't properly
down. Jane was told to sit farther forward in the saddle
and grip with her knees. 'And don't do it tensely, as if
it was hurting you!'

'How am I?' said Lolly who couldn't bear the
suspense any longer.

'Nice and straight,' said Mrs Lockett, 'but you must
keep your head up all the time, and your legs *still*. Still,
but not as if they were wired down. The leg position,'
she went on, 'is everything, and when you've got it
correctly you've got to make it second nature so that
you don't even have to think about it. In a Show you

can see people suddenly beginning to think, "Are my legs right?" and by then it's too late. The judges have noticed your indecision . . . Tom, I've told you before you can't use your hands properly if they're pressed against your thighs. Sit right up, shorten your reins, and put your legs back. Now you can all stop for a breather.'

'My, that was an eye-opener,' said Phil. 'I didn't realise we all had such faults.'

'You can never do too much simple riding in a circle,' said Mrs Lockett. 'Keep it up until you know that you simply can't go wrong, however long it goes on. You all ought to have a try at that every day. But we'll get along. Mount and prepare to trot.'

It was soon obvious that the trotting wasn't all that good. Phil, in front of me, seemed to be doing very nicely and I hoped I was too, as Mrs Lockett wasn't actually glaring at me, but Tom's pony was pulling and Lolly's trot occasionally became a canter and had to be corrected.

I noticed Jane bringing Nice Weather on to the bit with a sly kick which she certainly hoped her mother wouldn't see, while Mary held Agate so tightly that he had little freedom and his pace became an angry peck.

Many of these faults were such as only an experienced rider could notice, but they didn't escape Mrs Lockett's eagle eye. Everything was noted, and she made us all stop for the inevitable telling-off.

'Now off you go again,' she said, and after a couple of rounds she told us that we were all doing better.

'It's really quite stiff criticism,' said Mary. 'We should have got away with all those faults in an ordinary competition.'

'That's what I told you,' said Mrs Lockett. 'I'm out

for good riding, not passable riding. Now you can all prepare to halt.'

I'm sure that everybody knew they should use their legs to halt, but I was surprised to see one or two pulling on the reins – in fact I may have done it myself. Heaps of people do it in Shows, you'd be surprised.

Jane crowded Mary and got a black look, and Mrs Lockett shouted, 'Jane! For goodness' sake, relax your hands. Never whatever you do, hang on to your pony's head once he's halted. It looks thoroughly bad and the pony hates it. If I were a judge I'd disqualify anybody who did that . . . Everybody try again.'

We went on halting and moving off for ages; then we were told to cross our stirrups and ride round the school, first at a walk and then at a trot.

'Oh dear,' said Lolly loudly, 'have we *got* to do this? It makes me wiggle.'

'That's why you're doing it,' said Mary. 'To learn not to wiggle.'

'You wiggle too,' said Lolly. 'So does everybody.'

The next thing was to take back our stirrups and try some back-reining. Nobody was very good at this, I wasn't myself. Plum did it with extreme reluctance and a good deal of unnecessary quivering.

'This is something you have to do on every appearance in the show ring,' said Mrs Lockett. 'I can't think why you're making such heavy weather of it.'

'It's probably because you're watching us and we're trying too hard,' said Tom, 'though I'm never very sure of back-reining neatly. I wish I could be.'

'You must all go on practising until you *are* sure,' said Mrs Lockett. 'It should be as smooth a movement as any other. Every time you have a few minutes to spare, practise your back-reining or something you don't actually care to do. It's all too easy to practise

the things you enjoy, that's what mediocre people do.
Now you see how necessary this morning's work has
been, even if you do think you're being treated like
beginners.'

'Have we got to do this sort of thing every day?'
said Jane.

'Of course. In every odd quarter of an hour you
can bring your pony out here, mount him, and think
hard about the old-fashioned word Legs. It's the word
you've had shouted at you since the day you first
began to ride, and the word you're never to forget.'

Jane said she was already sick of the word Legs, and
what with her own two and the pony's four she felt
like an insect.

'And now,' said Mrs Lockett, 'you can each show
me in turn a few turns to left and right on the forehand.
You first, Phil.'

She was dissatisfied, of course, and we kept at it for a
long time. I think we all felt we were being done good
to. You can get into the way of taking for granted that
you can do all these things, which are elementary,
and suddenly you realise there is so much more to it
than just simple competency. We were going through
some real schooling, and couldn't help being better
for it. Actually by now we were all gasping with
weariness and being so strung up for so long.

'That'll do for now,' said Mrs Lockett at last. 'We'll
have lots more work before we've done.'

'Oh, am I exhausted!' said Mary.

'Me too,' said Tom.

'I'm in agony all over,' said Jane. 'I never felt like
this when I was learning to ride.'

'Don't forget,' said Mrs Lockett callously, 'that you
and Lolly have still got to clean up the yard before
lunch.'

'Oh crumbs!' said Lolly. 'That's the end. What are we – slaves?'

'We'll come and help you,' said Tom generously.

I went along and helped too, though they looked at me in a surprised way, and Mary said, 'You don't have to, you're a guest.'

'I'd rather,' I said. 'It's being part of the team.' I suppose they couldn't understand what was making me so unlike Amanda Applewood.

'By the way,' said Tom as we wandered at last towards the house, exhausted and grubby, 'I'd better warn you characters that if Mrs Wattington-Finch is one of the judges in the showing classes, she always asks you a question before she does the final placing, so you'd better swot up.'

Everybody shrieked, 'What sort of question?' and Tom said, 'Oh, something like, "what are leg bandages used for and how would you put them on?" When I was at Moss Hall gymkhana last month she asked the girl next to me who was sitting second, "How would you know if your pony had a temperature?" and the girl said, "I expect the groom would tell me," and Mrs W–F went pale green and sent her down from second place to fourth.'

'It's all in the veterinary book that Mother has got,' said Mary, 'and I think we ought to know more about it. Phil's jolly good at horse first-aid, but most of you aren't. As we're all aching so much, I vote we stop in this afternoon and do some swotting.'

'We might not get Mrs Whats-it,' said Jane hopefully.

'Whether we do or not,' said Phil, 'it won't hurt any of us to know what bandages are for, and how to put them on.'

'I've got a book upstairs called *The Horse in Sickness*

and in Health,' I said enthusiastically. 'I never go anywhere without it, and we could find questions in it and try them on each other.'

'Good show,' said Tom, looking at me more approvingly. 'If we swot up the temperature thing, and colic, and bad feet, those are the ones she's most likely to ask about, as they're the most likely to happen to ponies.'

'Jane says we might not *get* her,' said Lolly who hated swotting.

'*And* we might,' said Phil. 'Tom's quite right. If you did get her, and because you couldn't answer the question you got shoved out of first place into third or fourth, you'd feel pretty sick, wouldn't you?'

So after lunch we stayed in, and I got the book down, and we all sat round the dining-room table and asked each other questions, and it was rather fun. In spite of myself, I began to like the Locketts; and as I quite forgot for the time being that I was supposed to be Amanda, I realised that they were beginning to like me.

6 A few jumps

'Hurray, hurray, hurray!' sang Lolly at breakfast next morning. 'I know everything about horse first-aid. Old Whats-it can't floor me.'

'You mean, theoretically,' said Mary.

'What's theoretically?'

'Well you haven't actually done it. I mean if you did put the stable bandages on they'd be so lumpy they'd look like bunches of carrots. I think we all ought to practise, if it comes to that.'

'You shall, as soon as there's a wet day,' said Mrs Lockett. 'Meanwhile, this morning we'll try a little jumping.'

'And I've got a morning off, so I'll come and watch,' said Mr Lockett.

'I hope it won't be as gruesome hard work as yesterday,' said Jane, 'because I'm just one howling ache.'

'If you ache like that,' said Mrs Lockett, 'it's because you were doing everything wrong until yesterday, and not using the right muscles at all, so you ought to be thankful you've been shown how. It might even get you a placing on the day.'

Just then the postman knocked, and I muttered, 'I'll get it,' and rushed to the hall. Sure enough there was a letter for me, addressed to Miss Jill Crewe, and from Mummy. Phew! I thought, shoving it down my front. Saved again!

I brought the other letters back to the dining-room,

and Mary said, 'Gosh, Jill is coming on. Positively helping.' I thought it wouldn't be a bad idea to let them think I was steadily improving under their gentle refining influence.

After breakfast I went upstairs and read my letter in my room with the door shut, though it made me feel like the beautiful spy in films.

Mummy merely hoped I was having a good time and sent me ten pounds for expenses. I dashed her off a note telling her not to bother writing again as I should soon be back at the cottage in any case, thanked her for the welcome financial aid, and ran down to pop the letter on the hall table. After all, nobody would know who Mrs Crewe was!

In the dining-room Jane was saying, 'After yesterday's mass slaughter I can't help wondering what today has in store.'

'Plenty of hard work,' said Phil. 'We're going out to put up some jumps.'

'It'll be a change from schooling,' said Lolly.

'If it comes to that,' said Phil, 'Tom and I were both out walking a circle, back-reining, everything, before breakfast. It came a lot easier for yesterday's practice, but I didn't notice any of you girls.'

We went and got the ponies ready, then along to the paddock to see what was being prepared for us. Phil and Tom with Mr Lockett and the daily man were hard at work while Mrs Lockett looked on and gave instructions.

'I say, that course looks a bit weird, doesn't it?' said Mary to me. 'I suppose Mother knows what she's doing?'

We watched until the whole thing was completed, consisting of four jumps, and Mrs Lockett was satisfied. Then she said, 'Gather round while I explain. I think this is a pretty good set-up. There are just the four jumps, and they're only three-foot-six ones, but the point is they are staggered, so you'll have to use aids between each pair to get your ponies balanced and on the right leg. If you don't you won't be able to take the jump at all.'

'Oh, I call that fiendish,' said Mary. 'We'd never get anything like that on the day. They don't do anything quite as awful even at Wembley.'

'If you can jump this course you can jump any,' said Phil. 'It's a wow. What do you want to practise on, anyway? A few nice easy jumps for beginners? You ought to be able to do this course, you know the aids and it's just a matter of using your legs.'

Jane said, 'Oh listen to the pro!' Lolly said she hadn't ever done jumps that weren't in a straight line and hadn't a clue about legs, and surely that was the pony's business?

She seemed quite upset about the little course and jerked Gelert's bridle until he began to throw his head about, and Mrs Lockett told her to go in and put a martingale on him.

While she was away Phil said he would have first try.

'That's right,' said Mary ironically. 'You put 'em up, you try 'em out.'

Phil obviously thought this was a case of do or die. Having said so much he couldn't very well make a mess of things. After taking the first jump neatly he rather consciously collected Opal and gave exaggerated aids to show us how easy it was. Then he took the second jump and got over.

'He looked down to see if Opal had got her feet arranged,' said Lolly.

'Do you mind?' said Mrs Lockett. 'I'm doing the criticising here.'

Phil did a clear round, but Mrs Lockett said it was because he had an experienced pony who didn't need much help from him. Actually he had had very little contact with his pony's mouth.

'You're riding on too long a rein,' she pointed out as Phil waited for her comments, 'and though you did use your legs well, Opal could have had her head if she'd wanted to and everything might have gone wrong. Shorten your reins another time, and let your hands come forward at the take-off to give the necessary head. You'll get another chance later on – and all of you, ride your ponies as if you weren't completely sure that they understood you. Some day you might have to ride a strange pony, and that would be the test.'

'Oh, might we?' said Jane. 'How? When?'

'Once when I wasn't much older than you,' said Mrs Lockett, 'I was riding in a gymkhana when I heard someone saying that an owner had a lovely pony and nobody to jump him in the competition, as the girl who was going to ride him had been hurt. I pricked my ears up, and to make a long story short I found out the owner of the pony and asked, did she really want somebody to jump him, because I'd love to if she'd let me. She'd seen me ride before, and I suppose she trusted me, because she agreed to let me try. I had a wonderful ride on that pony, but because I didn't know his reactions or his disposition I really did have to ride him and give him all I'd got. Otherwise I'd have not only missed a treat but looked a fool as well.'

'Oh, what happened?' cried Lolly. 'Did you win?'

'I was second,' said Mrs Lockett. 'It could happen to one of you, and if it does I hope you'll be ready for it. You can't call yourself a rider if you're a one-horse person.'

'Of course we can all ride each other's ponies,' said Mary. 'We've done it often.'

'But not with what you'd call spectacularly good results,' said Tom. 'I'm sure I couldn't win a competition on Opal, or any pony I hadn't ridden regularly.'

My heart sank as I thought, That's just what I'm going to have to do in this Show! I would certainly have to ride with grim concentration.

'We're talking too much, and forgetting what we're here for,' said Mrs Lockett. 'Your go, Mary.'

Mary got over the first three jumps, though not too comfortably, but at the fourth she was right off balance and brought two rails down.

'Blow!' she said, coming up to us. 'That's a brute of a jump. You can't possibly get to it balanced, nobody could.'

'Rubbish,' said Mrs Lockett. 'You didn't even use your knees. You'll do it again later. Where's Jill and that perfect Plum? . . . Oh, there you are.' She looked at me critically and I dithered a bit. 'Now let's see your jumping. Off you go.'

I had been studying the jumps, and had the advantage of watching the first two and how they either coped or went wrong.

I got my knees well in and my heels hard down, shortened the reins, gave Plum the aids and hoped for the best. She was clever and keen, and went round nicely if a bit too carefully.

'Not bad,' said Mrs Lockett, 'only I would like to see you a bit more relaxed. If you're as tense on the day you'll never get round in the time.'

(No, but by then I hope I'll know Plum better! I thought. I can't take any chances with her yet.)

By now Jane was ready for the test, and off she went, with her reins too long in spite of all that had been said.

She cleared two of the jumps and scrambled over the other two, and returned festooned with all the brushwood she'd brought down.

'Coo! What a show!' said Phil. 'You simply lugged him round by the neck. Not a leg aid in sight.'

'I *did* use my legs – didn't I, Mary?' yelled Jane indignantly.

'Well, not very effectively,' Mary said. 'And you kept on looking back to see how you were doing. That's absolutely unpardonable.'

'I didn't,' said Jane.

'Yes, you did!' everybody shouted.

'If you don't realise that you kept looking back and looking down,' said Mrs Lockett, 'then you've got into a shocking habit, and you must break yourself of it. And I will not allow hauling on the reins. Some judges may pass it, but most of them won't. It's just what I was talking about, a high standard and a low one.'

Next Lolly went. Mrs Lockett arranged her properly in the saddle, well in the middle with her legs back.

'I feel funny,' said Lolly.

'Well, you're in the right position,' said Mrs Lockett, 'so hold it and all you've got to do is use the right aids. As soon as you land after the first jump, sit down firmly, left rein, right leg, and shift your weight to the left to bring you to the next jump.'

'I bet you anything I do it the wrong way round,' groaned Lolly.

However, she didn't do too badly at all, and though she brought part of each jump down, she did at least approach them balanced. This was more than Tom did, when he followed. Commodore was frisky, and swung round before each jump. Tom got very hot before he could persuade his pony to take three of the jumps – which he cleared with inches to spare – and he finally ran right out at the fourth.

'Lack of correct control,' said Mrs Lockett. 'Tom, I've never seen you ride so badly.'

'It's only these cock-eyed fences,' said Tom cheerfully. 'I'll manage next time.'

Just then Mr Lockett came out, and cried, 'How's everybody doing?' and everybody groaned and said, 'Ghastly!'

'Second round's coming up,' said Mrs Lockett. 'Come along, Phil.'

Everybody was much better this time, as well as more free, though Phil got told off for overconfidence and taking all the jumps too fast.

'There's no excuse for it,' said Mrs Lockett, 'even if they are low jumps and you feel sure of yourself. Just one hint of lack of control on the day, and in the general excitement you'll come to grief.'

Tom went next, on Commodore, who still danced a bit, but Tom looked after his balance much better and did a clear round.

'Phew!' he said, riding up to us. 'I wouldn't like to do that often!'

Plum again jumped nicely for me, and this time I felt more accustomed to her style and more free, though Mrs Lockett told me that I hadn't given her enough rein and on higher jumps she wouldn't have got over at all.

Jane and Lolly both got their legs tangled and came back in disgust while Mr Lockett roared with laughter at them. Mary jumped very well indeed and it was a pleasure to watch her. I couldn't resist saying, 'I say! You're awfully good.'

'Oh thank you!' she said, staring with surprise. 'That's something, coming from the great Amanda.'

'Oh, come off it!' I said, going red. 'I thought we were having an armistice.'

'I must say, you haven't thrown your weight about so much lately,' said Mary, 'so keep up the good work and we'll all stand by you.'

The morning was gone, and Mrs Lockett told us to go in and get ready for lunch. All through lunch we talked about nothing but the technicalities of jumping, and about courses we had jumped. After lunch, Jane said to me, 'Daddy's going to take us into town in the car to get something for Mary's birthday tomorrow. She'll be sixteen. Do you want to join?'

'Oh, yes please,' I said.

'We're all putting a pound in,' said Jane, 'and she wants a blue tie with crossed riding sticks on it, it's in the window at Wilson's sports shop, and it's just six pounds so if you join that makes the right amount.'

I felt rather flattered that they had included me. When it was time to start Mary insisted on coming too, which wasn't really included in the plan, but she said if we were going to town with Mr Lockett she didn't intend to miss anything.

The blue tie was in the window of the sports shop, so we all went in, only to find that they also stocked it in yellow, fawn, and red. This made things frightful, as Mary couldn't make up her mind which colour she wanted. She tried every one of them against herself, and still she couldn't make up her mind.

'Oh gosh, girls!' said Phil in disgust.

'Well, you needn't go on like that,' said Mary.

'You're such a fusspot about your stupid socks being just right. Which would you have anyway?'

'I can't understand you,' said Tom. 'You said yesterday you wanted the blue one. Well, *have* the blue one.'

'But the yellow one would look better with my gloves,' said Mary.

'Well, have the yellow one. Help! What do you want?'

Mary put on an expression of agony, and said, 'But I like the red one the best, actually, only it wouldn't go with anything I've got, and the fawn one is the same colour as my best pullover.'

Meanwhile Jane and Lolly were prancing about all over the shop, saying what they'd buy if they had wealth beyond the dreams of avarice, and there were quite a lot of things I'd have liked too. Phil and Tom both fancied a hacking coat that was sixty-five pounds, and argued about whether they dare ask to try it on, seeing they hadn't a hope of ever buying it. I think the man in the shop must have got pretty sick of us, he really was very patient.

After about half an hour Mary announced that she would have the blue tie after all.

'Well!' said Jane. 'After all that chopping and changing.' We came out into the street, and she added, 'I do think Mummy might have let us have those jumps in a straight line, then we'd have had a chance of bounding over them in style.'

'That wasn't her point,' said Phil. 'It's much more important when you're practising to take the jump the right way than to get over. It's the way you approach and take off that counts, isn't it, Mary?'

'Sure is,' said Mary.

'Oh, shucks!' said Jane. 'I just like to get over,

myself. And I don't know about you lot, but I'm hungry.'

'Well, let's have an ice,' said Mr Lockett.

I remembered the ten pounds that Mummy had sent me, and I said, 'Oh, do let me treat everybody to ices!'

'Is that Bighead I hear speaking?' said Mary. 'No thanks.'

'No, thank you,' said the others.

I felt very squashed, as I hadn't been showing off at all, and I said, 'I do think you're horrible. Why shouldn't I treat you, when I'm stopping with you and having everything?'

'Jill is quite right,' said Mr Lockett, 'and I think all you kids are very ungracious. Thanks very much, Jill. We'd all like to have ices with you.'

'OK,' said Phil. 'If Father says so. Thanks, Jill – Amanda – whatever you're called.'

So we went into a café and sat on red stools at the counter, and had ice cream or ice cream sodas, or whatever everybody chose.

Mr Lockett said that as it was Mary's birthday next day we'd go to the pictures for an extra treat. This led to the most gruesome argument. You know what it is like when a lot of people are going to the pictures, and everybody wants to go to a different one? The boys wanted to go to a Western, and Mary and Lolly wanted to go to a comedy, and Jane wanted to go and see Marlon Brando, and I rather fancied that myself only I daren't say so as I only seemed to get into trouble when I pitched in on anything. They stood in the street and argued and argued, and then Mr Lockett said, well, after all it was Mary's birthday and she ought to be allowed to choose; so suddenly everybody went extremely polite and unselfish towards Mary, and we all finished up by seeing the comedy and it was very good.

'Really, I'd as soon take a menagerie out,' said Mr Lockett. 'The time you all take making up your minds, we could do twenty things.'

7 Wings and flowerpots

Next morning we all wished Mary many happy returns, and she put on the blue tie, and also a lovely new watch that her parents had given her instead of the old one that she had worn all the time she was at school.

Jane said, 'Bags I get one of those for my fifteenth birthday!' and Mary said, 'Well, don't let me catch you putting your little pink fingers on this one.'

'Seeing it's a birthday,' said Lolly, 'perhaps we could have a day off that grim schooling, and just ride.'

'That grim schooling, as you call it,' said Mrs Lockett, 'is the one thing that is going to make our team better than the other teams on the day. So take it or leave it, it's up to you.'

'Hear, hear!' said Phil. 'So lay off, Lolly. You're only a kid, anyway, you don't understand.'

'I like that!' said Lolly. 'You were grumbling about so much schooling yourself.'

'Oh, we all grumble,' said Tom. 'It doesn't mean a thing.'

'I think we'll do a straightforward jumping course today,' said Mrs Lockett, 'so when you've done your chores, get out into the paddock and put up the jump with any trimmings you fancy.'

'Like wings and pots of flowers,' said Jane, 'like they had on the telly, at Wembley. They had pots of flowers all over the place, and that little horse, Nugget, was busting out all over the orchids.

'Well, you jolly well won't find any orchids to bust out over,' said Mary. 'But we could use the potted tobacco plants.'

'That's all you girls think about,' said Tom. 'Fancy jumps. Give me a good, plain wall to practise over. That's the jump that lets most people down, because your pony hates not to see the other side. I'm going to get Commodore so used to jumping the wall that I'll be sure of not getting any faults on the day.'

'Yes, at Wembley on telly,' said Jane, 'all the faults that were got seemed to be got at the wall, so Tom's right.'

'I wish you'd shut up about Wembley on telly,' said Lolly, 'when you know I wasn't allowed to sit up so late and see it. It was so mean.'

Jane stuck to her point, that you could learn an awful lot by watching the jumping at Wembley on television, if you weren't lucky enough actually to go there, and Phil said, 'That's just like you, Lazy! Sitting in an armchair watching other people jump is just about your line, when you'd do yourself far more good going twenty times over a three-foot brush fence and checking your own faults,' and the usual family argument broke out, until Mrs Lockett, who had been to the kitchen, came back and found us still sitting round the dining-room table and nothing done at all.

Naturally she was displeased, and said, Did we or did we not want to learn to jump properly, because there were still the chores to do and the jumps to put up.

The boys rushed off to the paddock with Mrs Lockett, and I – forgetting that I was Amanda – said,

'Come on, Jane and Lolly. It's Mary's birthday, so let's let her off chores today, and we'll clear away and make the beds, and dry the dishes for Mrs Place.'

'Jane blinked a few times, and then said 'OK.' Lolly, who liked housework, started piling up the breakfast plates, and Mary said, 'Gosh, that's nice of you, Amanda. You *are* improving.'

'Oh, call me Jill,' I said hastily, and nearly added, 'I'm not such a stinker as Amanda,' but saved myself in time.

By the time we finally got out to the paddock the jumps were nearly finished, and very nice they looked with their fresh paint. I envied the Locketts with all my heart for owning such a magnificent set of jumps, as the only ones I had ever owned – as you will know from reading my previous books – were self-made out of wood I had begged from farmers, or old chairs, or junk that my friends and I had laboriously collected and helped out with brushwood, and painted by ourselves.

There was a proper brush fence, a gate, a beautiful wall, a pair of parallel bars, a triple bar, and a double fence which acted as an in-and-out, and the whole set-up made a most professional jumping course.

Jane was all for going to fetch pots of plants from the greenhouse, but Mrs Lockett took a dim view of this, as apparently the pots of plants were Mr Lockett's joy and pride, and if they lost a single leaf in the fray he would have our blood for it. Well, nobody could guarantee – could they? – that those plants wouldn't lose a single leaf, in fact it was pretty obvious that they'd be lucky to have any leaves left at all; so we persuaded Jane to give up the idea.

'Now you can all do a free round,' said Mrs Lockett,

'and I'll criticise you. Go on, Phil – you first. You're the biggest.'

Phil cantered Opal in a large circle, until Mrs Lockett said Ting-a-ling, pretending to be the bell. Opal took the brush fence with plenty to spare, and cocked her ears as she looked at the next which was the gate, and rather narrow. Phil kept her perfectly straight, while he judged the distance. Opal went on slowly, I thought too slowly, and wouldn't have been surprised if she had refused, but she knew what she was doing and popped over neatly. We all let out our breaths.

Next came the black and white wall, at three-foot-six. Jane said, 'Opal likes the wall jump,' and apparently she did, because she went for it full tilt and simply sailed over. We clapped, because the jump was so well taken. The double fence came next and she did it very nicely. At the parallel bars her hind hooves gave a terrific rap, but nothing fell.

'Phil's always lucky,' gasped Lolly. 'Anything I touch always falls.'

Opal was now regarding the triple bar with a very suspicious eye as if she wasn't sure about the spread. Phil shortened the reins, and at the last moment slid his hands up her neck to give her freedom for the jump. She took off correctly, but misjudged the rail on the landing side, and down it came.

'Bad luck,' said Mary. 'I'm glad it wasn't a real competition, though I was nearly as excited as if it was.'

'That would be four faults,' said Mrs Lockett. 'Now you go, Mary.'

Mary on Agate took the brush fence with inches to spare.

'Look at that!' said Jane. 'She must have jumped five

foot.' The narrow gate didn't seem to worry Agate at all, but she got two refusals at the wall, and that was six faults.

'Just like I said,' said Jane. 'The wall's nearly always the snag. I'm going to practise at the wall like anything when I get a chance.'

When Mary got to the triple, it was obvious that Agate was excited and he began to pull madly. Mary was forced to let him increase his speed, though we could see her making a face. She obviously expected the worst, but over went Agate with an enormous bound which not only took him over the spread but landed him at least a yard clear. You should have seen Mary's face! We all burst out laughing, and the boys cheered ironically.

'Six faults!' said Mary, riding up to us. 'And I thought I was going to bring the lot down at that last jump.'

'Too many oats,' said Lolly. 'That's what's the matter with Agate.

'Agate was certainly overexcited,' said Mrs Lockett. 'You'll have to watch that, Mary. There's no excuse for a rider of your experience letting her pony get out of control.'

'I wouldn't mind how much mine got out of control,' said Lolly, 'if he'd take jumps like that.' We all began to giggle, but Mrs Lockett looked at us severely, and said, 'That's a silly remark, and you all know it.'

Soon Tom was up and cantering towards the first jump which he did easily, and also the next which was the gate. He scattered two bricks at the wall, and then didn't turn quickly enough for the double fence so that he approached it at an angle and reaped two more faults, but he cleared both the parallel bars and the triple.

'You know what happened at the wall, don't you?' said Mrs Lockett. 'Commodore was off the bit and dropped her hind legs. And you must watch your turns. Are you ready to go now, Jill?'

Plum was in the nicest of moods, and had watched the other ponies jumping with great interest, obviously anticipating her turn. I didn't want to do *too* well, but it was one of those days when one can't make a mistake. Plum timed her fences beautifully and sailed over, though we were lucky at the triple because I felt she was dropping her heels too soon and she must have cleared the down-side bar by a hair's breadth.

'Very good,' said Mrs Lockett, 'but don't get over-confident. That's likely to be your trouble, Jill.'

(Oh no, it isn't! I thought. Overconfidence is the last thing that'll trouble me. How little you know!)

'Fluke,' I said modestly. 'I could easily have messed the whole thing up.'

Next came Jane, and, trying too hard, she went for the course with tremendous dash, like somebody in a Western film. Anything she cleared she overcleared, and finished up with eight faults and a telling-off.

'The only jump you did passably was the first one,' said Mrs Lockett. 'After that it was a stampede, and you deserved sixteen faults, not eight. You're not riding in a circus. What saved you was that your pony has lots of spring and courage, but you shouldn't trade on those things.'

Jane wasn't pleased, and said, 'Well, that's better than being afraid to let him go, always tugging and jerking at his mouth to bring him back to hand.'

'Oh, really!' said Mary. 'There is a happy medium.'

Jane, who hadn't heard the phrase before, opened

her eyes wide and said, 'What's a happy medium?' and we all giggled, which restored good temper.

It was Lolly's turn, and she jumped with care, but her pony didn't like the wall, refused it three times, and swung away.

'What ought I to do now?' yelled Lolly, red-faced.

'Go round it,' said Mrs Lockett, 'and try the next jump.'

'No I won't,' said Lolly. 'I'll jump this beastly wall.'

And she did! She also jumped the double fence, correcting Gelert's stride like an experienced rider – and the parallel jump too, and went on to take the triple without turning a hair.

'Good old Lolly!' shouted Tom. 'Did you ever see anything like that?'

'Apart from the refusals at the wall,' said Mary in a dazed voice, 'she hasn't got any faults at all.'

This had evidently been apparent to Lolly also, as she now came up to us at a gallop, standing in the stirrups and screaming, 'Aren't I super? No actual faults.'

'You wait till I get hold of you, show-off!' muttered her brother, grinding his teeth.

I thought it was time I said something a bit Amanda-like, so I said airily, 'As a matter of fact, I was the only one who did a clear round.'

I was sorry to have to make myself say this, as I was getting to like the others and couldn't help thinking how, under happier circumstances – as they say in books – we could have had a marvellous time together. So it made me very uncomfortable when they quite excusably glared at me with loathing.

Mrs Lockett said coldly, 'We're all well aware of your achievements, Jill, and the fact that you have a perfect pony. But there's danger even for you – in fact, particularly for people like you. You get a pony that knows its job, and you take advantage of that and rely on the pony until you can't even call yourself a rider; you might as well be on a bus. I don't say you do it, but you could. The minute you cease to have your pony fully collected, and something unforeseen happens, you'll be in a shocking mess, and serve you right!'

I felt myself going red, because of course I thoroughly agreed with everything Mrs Lockett said. For the minute I wished Plum at the bottom of the sea, and would have given anything to see the dark pricked ears of one of my own ponies in front of me instead of those grey ones.

'Yes, I know,' I mumbled.

'Well, come along everybody,' said Mrs Lockett. 'We'll have the jumps lowered, and you can cross your stirrups.'

A few people groaned, and Mrs Lockett added, 'And please don't let anybody go galloping round the field flapping their legs.'

We all jumped without stirrups, and then we bigger ones knotted the reins and jumped with our arms folded.

'Not as good as I'd wish,' said Mrs Lockett, just when we were thinking rather well of ourselves. 'You've all got your legs too far forward; and do for goodness' sake, Tom, open your fingers and lighten your hands a bit. You look like a disappointed jockey losing the nursery stakes.'

We giggled, and Mary said, 'I'm sure that's enough for the morning, Mother, we're all aching, and these kids have got to have enough strength to rub their ponies down properly.'

'I always do!' said Lolly.

'I bet no other team is working like us,' said Phil. 'I know the Rectory team aren't. Do you think we're overdoing it, and might get stale?'

Mrs Lockett gave him a withering look, and Tom said, 'Don't take any notice of him, he's a lazy lout. Now me, I don't care how hard I work as long as I win something on the day.'

'Wouldn't it be marvellous,' said Jane dreamily, 'if our team got first, second, and third in heaps of the events?'

'Just a bit too marvellous,' said Phil.

'There's no reason why you shouldn't,' said Mrs Lockett. 'I hope you do, so long as you don't boast about it.'

We led our ponies away to rub down, and I said to Mary, 'Oh, I do envy you that wonderful set of jumps you've got!'

Mary stared at me, and said, 'You don't have to flatter us, you know. Prue Kelly, who's at school with you, told us that you had a set of jumps at home good enough for Richmond Horse Show.'

'Well, it's not true,' I said.

'Prue Kelly said you told her so yourself.'

I felt like saying, Oh blast Prue Kelly! And blast Amanda! Because at that moment I longed to be Jill Crewe, and I was thinking of my own field at home and the funny jumps that my friends and I had collected together, and I knew that the Locketts would have enjoyed hearing about them.

Then Jane said a terrifying thing. She said, 'Prue Kelly's coming round this afternoon to borrow a book about birds. She's not exactly a friend of ours, but her brother wants it and I said we'd lend it to him. So you two can natter about school, if you want to.'

I went cold all over. Thank goodness I had had

a bit of warning! Supposing I hadn't known, and had floated downstairs to find this strange girl glaring at me and gasping, 'But that isn't Amanda Applewood!'

My brain worked like lightning, as it sometimes does in an emergency and sometimes doesn't. Fortunately in this case it did.

I said in my Amanda-voice, 'Well, Prue Kelly's going to be unlucky, because I'm going out with Plum by myself all the afternoon.'

'I don't suppose she'll cry her eyes out,' said Jane.

Directly after lunch, which I didn't enjoy much, I disappeared and flew to get Plum. The others all thought I was crazy, as it was a very hot afternoon and they felt like lazing, but I was terrified that at any moment this Prue Kelly might appear.

Plum didn't look too pleased, either, but I saddled her up and rode briskly away. Only when I was out of sight of the house did I slacken pace, give Plum her head, and feel safe to amble along a grassy track. It was getting hotter every minute and the flies were a nuisance. When I got to a copse I was glad to ride into it and get down and sit under a tree, cooling off while Plum nosed the soft thin grass, but it grew boring and I wished I had had the sense to bring a book. It was only half-past two.

'Come on, Plum,' I said at last, and up I got and walked her slowly along a lane between the cornfields, fast turning gold. At least I felt I was getting to know her better, and that was something, though she was probably fed up with the sight of me! Then we crossed a common that was peppered all over with rabbit warrens, and Plum hated that. I knew by now she thought I was quite mad, and if she could have talked would have said, 'Why can't we either do something useful, or go home?'

It was the longest, most boring afternoon I had ever spent, the hours crawled; then when it got to around five o'clock I became terribly hungry. I thought, Hurray, it's teatime, then realised that I daren't go back as they would be sure to ask Prue Kelly to stay to tea!

About an hour later, wondering whether I was destined to starve to death, suddenly all went black, up came a grim wind, and down came the rain in a torrent. I rode Plum under some trees and waited, but the rain came sloshing through the leaves and soon we were both soaking. Plum turned her head and fixed me with a horrified, accusing eye. It was no use, we'd have to go home.

Sopping wet and feeling like nothing on earth, I arrived at the stable yard, took Plum into her loose box and began to rub her down. She was thoroughly dejected and I had awful visions of her getting pneumonia – all due to Prue Kelly. I dried her as best I could and put on her rug, and it took ages owing to my own weak and famished condition. The tack was in an awful state, but I rubbed it as dry as I could and thought I'd get round to cleaning it tomorrow.

It was past seven o'clock, and I was just wondering gloomily if I dare go to the house, or if they had asked Prue Kelly to stay the evening and play Canasta, when who should appear but Mrs Lockett. That's torn it! I thought.

'Good gracious, Jill!' she said. 'Wherever did you get to? You don't mean to say you were out in all that rain?'

'I got caught,' I said feebly. 'I was rather a long way away.'

'And I suppose you forgot all about tea!'

I thought, *au contraire* – because for the last two hours I had thought about little else, but I didn't say anything.

'Is Plum all right?' she said. 'Have you rubbed her thoroughly? She'd better have a hot mash. I'll see to it. It really was rather silly of you to drift off on your own like that.'

'I can see to her food –' I began, nearly ready to eat a handful of oats myself; but Mrs Lockett said, 'The best thing you can do is to go straight upstairs, have a hot bath, and get into bed. I'll send somebody up with your tea.'

I jumped at the excuse of not having to meet the others, and in about ten minutes – having slunk up the stairs silently – I was in the bath, and in another ten, in bed.

Presently the door opened and in came Jane with a tray. I ran my eye over it, and it certainly looked very nice; sandwiches, hot buttered toast, strawberry jam, and a big pot of tea.

'Mother said you looked like a drowned rat,' said Jane.

'I'm all right now,' I said. 'Thanks awfully for the tea.'

'Prue Kelly asked where you were,' said Jane, 'and we said we didn't know, you'd just drifted off into the blue, and she said it was typical of you, everybody at school knew you were hopeless.'

'I suppose she stayed to tea?' I said.

'Oh no,' said Jane, 'she only stayed about ten minutes altogether.'

Well! I thought, gnashing my teeth on the toast. All

that suffering for nothing! I decided that there wasn't much to be said for a life of sordid deception; and though it goes down all right in films, *anybody* can have it so far as I'm concerned!

8   The good old days

On Sunday we went to church, and as we came out some other boys and girls said 'Hello', to the Locketts.

'That's the opposition,' said Mary to me. 'They're in the Rectory team, and they're said to be good.'

'The Hare girl's pretty hot,' said Phil. 'She's the vet's daughter, and she's had about eight firsts this season in various gymkhanas.'

'Pooh!' said Jane. 'Potty little Saturday afternoon gymkhanas with a lot of kids and beginners.'

'There's one thing you oughtn't to do,' said Tom, 'and that's to underrate the opposition. At Morwood Hill last month I thought they all looked a dim lot, in fact I said to myself, What a bunch of drips! and believe me or believe me not, I didn't win a single event.'

'Yes, that's true,' I said. 'I learnt that a long time ago.'

Mary said, 'Gosh, you've gone very modest all of a sudden.'

It rained all the afternoon, so we stayed in and played Monopoly, and Mrs Lockett said it was a good idea to give the ponies a day's rest anyway.

'I'm going to swot up the book tonight,' Mary said. 'I've got the possibility of Mrs Wattington-Finch in my hair. Judy Philips told me yesterday that she was judging at a gymkhana last week, and she suddenly flung at a girl who was sitting first, "What's a bit jointed?" – just like that! Well, honestly the girl couldn't think. I mean, who could? It's Mrs W–F's idea of being funny. Why on earth couldn't she have said, "What's the correct name for a jointed bit?" Everybody knows it's a snaffle. But no, she has to put it, "What's a bit jointed?" Ha, ha, ha!'

Everybody groaned.

'Oh, shut up about Mrs What's-it,' said Tom. 'You're giving us the creeps. If you had to learn the answers to all her possible silly questions you'd be up the wall. I'm going to trust to luck.'

'I'm going to jolly well trust I don't flipping well get her,' said Lolly.

'You know you're not allowed to say flipping,' said Jane. 'And hurry up with whatever you're doing, because it's you and me to do the feeds tonight.'

The next morning Mrs Lockett said it would be a good idea to do some games to loosen us up, and we all thought it would be fun.

'It'll give the ponies a rest from all that school-ing,' said Jane. 'Too much schooling is said to ruin a pony.'

'Any excuse for laziness!' said Mrs Lockett.

We did a little trotting to loosen up the ponies and then had a wild gallop round the field, while the boys yelled something that they had heard in a film called *The Rebel Yell*, which was supposed to be what the southern soldiers yelled in the American Civil War, only it sounded like sick cows and not like the film at all, Mary said.

We then had a picking-up-handkerchiefs race, the handkerchiefs being bits of rag laid on the grass, and only we big ones were allowed to do it because Mrs Lockett said that letting Jane and Lolly loose with spiked sticks was asking for death. We went in turns, and the idea was to pick up as many handkerchiefs as possible in 120 seconds; they were well scattered over the field so you had to canter and be nippy on your turns. I got nine handkerchiefs, and Mary got ten. Tom got only four, as he was much too dashing and dropped most of those he spiked, and Phil was an old hand at it and got thirteen.

Jane and Lolly wanted a dressing-up race, and we thought this was rather young of them. I mean, it is not the sort of thing one chooses to do on a warm summer afternoon, after leaving one's horsy infancy behind, but they wanted it so we said they could do it by themselves.

They went and collected piles of odd garments from the downstairs cloakroom – even a winter overcoat each – and dumped them at the bottom of the field; then they came back to the start and mounted and galloped down to the clothes.

When they had got all the garments on they looked like fat cocoons and couldn't even mount their ponies. We nearly collapsed with laughing when they kept flopping back to earth. They had to take some of the clothes off, and in the end Lolly got home two seconds before Jane, only Jane said it wasn't fair because Lolly had abandoned the overcoat, which was the heaviest garment, while Jane had only shed things like pullovers.

After that we all did a relay race.

Plum didn't seem to care about it. She was happy and I dropped the stick when taking it over from Tom, and as I was the only one who *did* drop it I felt humiliated.

'You'll have to do better on the day,' Phil said. 'We've entered for the relay race as a team.'

This depressed me. I had awful visions of letting the team down, and if you can think of anything worse than dropping the stick in a relay race competition, with millions of eyes upon you, I can't.

Next we had a break and went into the kitchen for biscuits and lemonade. We were all pretending to be cowboys coming home from a rodeo, and Mrs Place said, a little more of this and she'd be round the bend. It reminded me of home, where the simple pleasures of horsy people were likewise misunderstood.

After the break Jane and Lolly wanted Musical Mats, but we couldn't have it because the battery of the record-player had died on us, so we put up the bending poles and practised seriously, and finished up with a Gretna Green which Tom and Lolly won, as they had been doing it together all their lives.

By now we were gasping, and the ponies had had enough. Mrs Lockett said we ought each to know by now which was our weak point in games, but there were plenty of evenings left to practise.

'There aren't a lot of evenings,' said Mary gloomily 'and we've all got so many weak points. I wonder if other people are working as much as we are?'

'If they're not,' said Phil, 'we ought to get some advantage from it on the day.'

'And if they are,' said Tom, looking glum, 'they'll probably be miles better.'

'Oh you are a cheerful lot!' said Jane. 'With all the work that Mother's putting in on us, we'll never dare to come home if we don't win.'

This set the Locketts off talking about what they'd do if they didn't dare to come home from the Show, such as joining the Navy (the boys), trying to get into television (Jane and Lolly), and going to work in somebody's stable (Mary). I knew what I'd do, without saying so! Set off home for Chatton, and beg my bread if necessary on the way.

When I got Plum back to the loose box to rub her down I discovered that somebody had taken away my brushes and grooming things. Jane admitted that she had 'borrowed them', and when found they were all mixed up with the others, and dirty.

At that moment I felt much more like Amanda Applewood than Jill Crewe, and flung myself into a furious row with Jane. My riding hat flew off, and Jane – backing away from me – sat down on it and squashed it, and it was picked up covered with bits of dirty straw; and Jane said I had bitten her, which was quite untrue as I don't do things like that.

'You horrible biter!' said Jane.

'I did not bite!' I shouted.

'Oh, pipe down, you two,' said Phil.

'It's Jane's fault,' I said bitterly. 'It's the most disgusting thing a person can do, taking another person's tack without asking, and messing it all up.'

'You needn't be so mean,' said Tom. 'Just because your pony's so perfect, your tack isn't sacred or anything.'

'Well, Jane will have to sort it out from the rest, and clean it,' I said furiously. I was really upset about the brushes, because they were not mine but Amanda's, and when I finally handed them over I didn't want her to think I treated them like rubbish.

'All right, all right,' said Mary. 'Jane will. Only you needn't have been so touchy in the first place. If you'd asked Jane decently she'd have apologised for taking the stuff. Say you're sorry, Jane, for goodness' sake, or we'll never get any lunch – and you'd better say you're sorry too, Jill, for going at Jane like a tiger.'

Jane said she was sorry, and so did I – just to keep

the peace – but I added that I'd clean the stuff myself as I didn't fancy Jane's idea of cleaning tack, and this didn't make me any more popular!

Eventually the row simmered down and we had lunch.

In the afternoon Mr Lockett said he would take us for a walk, to see the house and grounds of Lord Whoever-it-was that he was agent to. This proved very interesting. There were wonderful woods which Mr Lockett said were at one time stocked with noble pheasants for the sport of the idle rich, but now of course that was the kind of thing that few could afford; and there was parkland which was let out for ley to farmers, as all the estate had to be self-supporting in these hard times for landowners. At the back of the enormous house there had been stabling for sixteen horses, but now it was only used as garges.

'What a let-down,' said Phil. 'If ever I'm a million-aire I'll buy a place like this, and restore it to stables.'

'That's a dream!' said Mr Lockett. 'Of course, in the old days all the family hunted, and they also kept pairs of matched carriage horses. You children don't know what it feels like to ride in a carriage. It's a lovely smooth, gliding sensation, I can't describe it. I haven't ridden in one since I was a kid.'

'I expect the only people who know what it feels like are the Royal Family,' I said.

'It must have been horrid driving in stage coaches,' said Mary. 'So stuffy and springless.'

'And expecting a highwayman to come and hold you up and rob you,' said Tom.

'There's an old family coach here, that they keep as a curiosity,' said Mr Lockett. 'I'll show it to you. It's nearly two hundred years old.'

The coach looked as if it weighed twenty tons, it

was very elaborate and painted green and gold. The coachman's box was extremely high, and there was a place for two footmen at the back. It had been drawn by six horses.

'I'd love to drive it,' sighed Phil, 'but I expect it would fall to bits if it was moved.'

'Oh, please, can we get inside?' begged Lolly.

'Well, only one at a time,' said Mr Lockett. 'If this thing drops to pieces I'll probably be sent to prison.'

We all got into the coach in turns, and actually it felt beautifully comfortable, with soft velvet seats and fat cushions swathed in cotton covers to preserve them.

'Some other people I know have got an old carriage,' said Mary, 'and once when they got inside the cushions burst and a lot of rats came gushing out.'

'You should have told us that before we went in,' I said, 'and we wouldn't.'

Mr Lockett then showed us some loose boxes where all the woodwork was solid mahogany with real brass fittings, and above were grooms' quarters, now deserted and crumbling with broken roofs.

'It's very sad,' he said, 'to see the relics of departed glory.'

'Like in museums,' said Lolly. 'Is Lord What's-it about a hundred years old?'

'Oh, no,' said Mr Lockett. 'We're talking about his grandfather's day.'

Tom said it must have been nice to be a lord a hundred years ago, and Mr Lockett said, 'You're telling me!'

It seemed that the present lord and his wife had five children, and they lived in just a small corner of the house. There was a picture gallery we could see if we liked. We did like, and Mr Lockett took us inside. We all said, 'Phew!' because a lot of the pictures were of horses belonging to the family, and they were marvellous. Apparently in those days they used to engage artists to paint portraits of the horses as well as of the ancestors.

All the horses in the paintings looked blue-blooded and noble, and they had their names underneath. The one I liked was called Mountain Fire of Chanados which I thought was terrific, and in the picture he was just about to jump a river which looked thirty feet across, though doubtless this was a bit of poetic fancy. Lolly started to cry, because the picture she liked was of a pony's head, and underneath it said, 'Tillie, a child's darling, died March 4th 1819, greatly missed.'

She said it was so beautiful and so sad she'd never forget it, and if ever she had another pony she'd call it Tillie-a-child's-darling, and Tom said that if she did it would probably die too, and she simply howled with crying.

She made such a din that a door at the end of the gallery opened and a woman came in, and she turned out to be Lord Whatever-it-was's wife. She was awfully nice, and said she knew just how Lolly felt as she had often cried over that picture too. Then she went and fetched some chocolates to console Lolly, and we all got consoled also.

We stayed for ages looking at the pictures of horses, and Mr Lockett pointed out some ancestors too, but Phil said he'd rather have horses than ancestors any day, and Lady What's-it began to laugh and said that on the whole she agreed with him. She then asked us if we were riding in the Show, and we said yes, we were a team of six, and she said, 'Good gracious, Mr Lockett, I never dreamed you had such an enormous family!'

Mr Lockett then had to explain about three of us being his, and two cousins, and then he said, 'And this is Amanda Applewood, from Chatton, who's making up our six.'

Lady I-forget-her-name looked at me in a puzzled sort of way, and said, 'I'm sure I've seen you riding somewhere.'

I went scarlet because I didn't know whether she meant that she'd seen *me* riding, or that she'd seen Amanda riding, and whatever she meant it terrified me.

She said, 'Heavens, dear, don't be so bashful,' and the others looked surprised. I had merely forgotten for the time being my guilty secret, and now it was back with me again.

9 Tom comes to grief

You must not be allowed to forget that in between the things I am telling you about we were doing schooling, and schooling, and schooling. I cannot keep on describing this, and you would be bored if I did, but there was never a day but we went out, if it was only for half an hour, to practise all the ordinary, monotonous things like walking, halting, back-reining, diagonal aids, and having the pony's feet where they ought to be without looking down to see – you know them. We let the ponies walk out and collected them, over and over again. We trotted and changed legs at the canter, and did figures of eight, and led out in hand, and mounted and sat still and dismounted, and unsaddled without making heavy weather of it.

It got to the stage when you daren't be seen about the place doing nothing for a quarter of an hour without Mrs Lockett descending upon you and saying, 'Just time for a few minutes' schooling.' She certainly did make us work, and in between grumbling we realised that it was a very good thing.

I couldn't say that I hadn't ample opportunity for getting to know Plum, and I soon became used to her. In some ways she was what you might call perfect, but in others I found her slightly more stupid than my own ponies, which surprised me. She had lots of spirit and temperament, and I wouldn't care for a pony who hadn't; it was just a matter of learning her likes and dislikes and adapting my ways to hers, and hers to mine. I felt a great deal happier about riding her in the Show.

One morning at breakfast Tom said, 'I think we ought to go out and do some ditch-jumping. I feel like it.'

Jane put her elbows on the table and said, 'I wonder why Tom always gets silly ideas at mealtimes?'

Lolly flew to the defence of her brother, and shouted, 'It isn't a silly idea at all, and I'm all for it.'

Mrs Lockett looked thoughtful.

'Really, Lolly,' she said, 'I don't know that I'm anxious for *you* to do ditch-jumping. I don't think you're experienced enough.'

'But I am!' Lolly wailed. 'Honestly, I'm frightfully experienced, Aunt Phyllis, and I'll have to do it in the Hunter Hurdle race; it's important because whatever I win or get placed in has bonus marks.'

'That's true,' said Phil, 'so you'd better let her do it, Mother. It doesn't matter if she breaks her neck so long as we get the bonus marks.'

'Hear, hear!' said Jane. 'Perhaps if she breaks her neck in the noble cause of equitation they might give our team a special bonus. That would be something.'

'You are a cold-blooded lot!' said Tom. 'If you want to murder somebody's sister, Phil, try one of your own. And if Lolly breaks her neck ditch-jumping in the hunter race, she won't be there to win anything in the afternoon, will she? The team would look pretty thin without her. You didn't think of that, did you, Clever Little Jane? But you needn't worry about Lolly, she's hot at ditch-jumping, because round about where we live there are plenty of ditches. You can't go out without having to jump them.'

'And they're enormous,' said Lolly. 'Yards wide. Wider than anything they'll have in the competition.'

'Well, let's get back to where all this started,' said Tom. 'Please can we try some ditch-jumping, Aunt Phyllis?'

'You wear me down,' said Mrs Lockett in a resigned sort of voice. 'You can jump anything you like only don't blame me for the consequences.'

'Hurray!' said Tom, gulping down his last bit of toast. Let's go and jump that ditch in Mead Bottom. There's a good grassy hill down to it, and we can gallop and pretend we're Italian cavalrymen.'

'I shall be there,' Mrs Lockett said grimly; 'and we'll see about Italian cavalrymen.'

Mary was clattering the plates together, and I began to help her.

'I think it's the limit,' she said, 'the way you others always leave everything for Jill and me to do. As for Jane, you'd think she'd been born to a palace full of slaves, the way she ignores the chores.'

Tom gave a yelp, and began to prance round the table with the tea-cosy on his head, chanting,

> Jane scores
> When she ignores
> The beastly chores
> Because they are bores.

'Some mothers do have them!' said Phil.

'Well, I made my bed before breakfast,' said Jane.

'Made it?' screamed Lolly. 'Made it! She just threw the bedclothes over and didn't even straighten the sheet. She deserves to get corns, lying on it.'

'Just listen to me,' said Mrs Lockett. 'Jane, go upstairs and make your bed properly, and then dust the hall. Mary and Jill, clear the table and peel the potatoes for lunch. Lolly, lay the table for lunch. And you two boys, go and get the ponies ready – *all* the ponies.'

When we had all done our chores we met outside. It was a sparkling sunny morning, and the ponies looked lovely. It really was a beautiful sight to see them, Opal and Agate, Nice Weather and Commodore, and Gelert and Plum. Plum gave me a rather doubtful look, as if she wondered what she was in for now, a sort of 'Wot – more games?' look.

Mrs Lockett was riding Blue Witch, a lovely mare that they were stabling for some friends who were away.

We all mounted and clattered out into the sunny lane. A woman who was going by with a little boy said, 'Look, dear, a riding school.'

Phil said under his breath, 'That's what you think!'

Tom led the way, and when we got to the spot he had chosen he said, 'There you are! Isn't it just the job?'

'Gosh!' said Mary. 'I'm not riding down there.'

It was a steep sandy bank with some coarse grass on it, and at the bottom was a meandering brook about four feet across.

'I don't think it's very suitable,' said Mrs Lockett. 'It's too steep, and it looks loose, and you'd never get anything like that in the competition.'

'Oh, Aunt Phyllis, it's dead easy,' said Tom.

'OK, I'll have a go,' said Phil, and put Opal at it. She more or less slithered down the hill, and cleared the brook at the bottom. Phil grinned back at us, and put his thumbs up.

'I'm not doing it,' said Lolly.

'I am,' said Jane.

'Oh no, you're not,' said Mrs Lockett.

'But it's just like the Italian cavalry did in that film.'

Actually I was wishing I had Rapide there, because I had done this cavalry stuff with him often on steeper banks than this, and it was just his cup of tea; but I didn't feel I should risk it on Plum. In fact Plum was already rolling her eyes dramatically and shying away from the slope.

'If Phil can do it, I can,' said Mary, and she put Agate – who was a tough pony and gave the impression of being ready for anything – at the slope. Agate didn't seem to mind it, he had very strong hindquarters and got Mary down quicker than Phil's pony had done it, finishing up with a swiping kind of jump that took him well over the brook. Mary rode round and came back with the air of a hard woman to hounds.

'Go on, Jill,' she said. 'I wouldn't let Plum shy away from a little thing like that and get away with it.'

I felt I had to go. Plum was too good a pony to refuse what she was being encouraged to do, and down we went very cautiously – Plum silently protesting with every hair – reached the bottom and took the jump from practically a standstill. Her hind legs finished in the water and I got more than a sprinkling.

When I joined the others Tom said, 'I call that a mingy exhibition for a perfect pony.'

'I wasn't giving an exhibition,' I pointed out. 'I had to do it, but I wasn't taking any risks with Plum's legs.'

'Well, I hope she looks a bit more willing on the day,' said Tom; and Phil said, 'We shan't get anything like that on the day.'

Mrs Lockett said she would have a try, in fact Blue Witch seemed anxious to do so and for all we knew

had been brought up on this sort of thing in the
remote Apennines. She went down very well indeed
and cleared the brook with a couple of feet to spare.

'Fancy daring to do that on somebody else's horse!'
said Jane.

(You little know! I thought, with what they call in
books a sardonic smile.)

Jane said she wanted to have a try, and why
shouldn't she? Supposing for instance that one day
her life depended on doing a thing like that, and she
couldn't because she'd never had any practice?

'Well, wait till I've been,' said Tom. 'I thought of
all this, and I haven't had a turn yet.'

He set off with considerable dash.

'Don't show off!' shouted Phil.

Commodore was down on his haunches looking
extremely uncomfortable, the next minute the whole
bank seemed to give way and the pony and Tom began
to roll over and over to the bottom, and ended up in
the brook.

Jane and Lolly let out a shattering shriek. Phil,
Mary, Mrs Lockett and I left our ponies and went
scrambling down the slope which was now a mound
of loose sliding sand.

By the time we got to the bottom Commodore
was struggling to get on his feet in the water, with
his saddle upside down under his tummy and the
reins tangled round his legs. Phil got hold of him,
and we went on to Tom who was lying quite still
in the water.

It was shallow, and we dragged him out between
us on to the bank. In a minute he opened his eyes and
began to move.

'Is anything broken?' said Mary. 'We'd better be
careful. Tom, are you all right?'

'I'm all right,' said Tom. 'I just feel funny.'

We all helped him to get up and he stood leaning against Mrs Lockett.

'You're bright, aren't you?' said Phil. 'I expect you're concussed and you won't be able to ride again for ages.'

Tom said, 'Curse! Is Commodore all right?'

'I don't know,' said Phil. 'He's had a nasty shake-up. I'll try to walk him in a minute and then we'll see. You were an idiot, Tom.'

'It's no good saying that,' said Mrs Lockett. 'The mischief's done now, so let's try and get home and see what the damage is.'

'The damage will probably be that Tom's out of the team,' said Phil gloomily. 'We've had it.'

Tom looked very sick and white, and began to shiver in his wet clothes.

'Come on,' said Mrs Lockett. 'Don't let's waste time. You try leading Commodore, Phil; if he'll go, get him home, and we'll manage Tom between us.'

Phil encouraged the pony to walk a little, and we were thankful to see that he could do that.

'What happened?' shrieked Jane and Lolly, suddenly appearing. 'Are they dead?'

'I'm all right,' said Tom crossly, making an effort to stand by himself, 'so don't make silly remarks. But I'm jolly wet.'

'Commodore looks horrible,' said Jane. 'What if he can't be in the Show?'

As that was what we were all thinking, we glared at Jane for putting it into words.

Phil gently encouraged Commodore who consented to move on slowly, still shivering and rolling his eyes; Mrs Lockett and Mary supported Tom, and I went back to pick up his hat which was floating about in the brook. We got back to where the ponies were, and three of us hoisted Tom up on Opal.

'Can you manage?' said Mrs Lockett. 'Shall Mary lead you?'

Tom said, 'Not likely!' but the next minute he shut his eyes and looked dizzy, and didn't protest when Mary took the bridle.

'You get along home,' said Phil. 'Commodore can walk all right, so I'll follow you slowly.'

It seemed a long way home, and when we finally got back we felt a dismal crowd after having set off so gaily.

Mrs Lockett took Tom straight into the house for a hot bath and bed. The rest of us began to unsaddle the ponies.

Mary said, 'If our team's out of the Show it's all Tom's fault, and I'll never forgive him.'

'He'll be all right,' said Lolly. 'He's had worse tosses than that and he was all right in no time.'

'But not if he's concussed,' said Jane. 'It wasn't like an ordinary toss; he and Commodore rolled over and over.'

'Oh, don't keep talking about it!' said Lolly angrily. 'I tell you, he'll be all right. And if it comes to that, Tom was only being a good sport, which is more than any of the rest of you were.'

'Sport!' yelled Jane. 'He was just being an idiot.'

Lolly picked up a dandy brush and threw it at Jane, and the next minute they were fighting like mad.

Mary went into the house and I turned the ponies into the field. When I got back Jane and Lolly were still at it, hammer and tongs. They only stopped when suddenly Phil appeared, leading Commodore slowly in.

'Do you mind if I put him in Plum's loose box

for now?' said Phil to me. 'Then I'll go and phone the vet.'

I said I shouldn't be surprised if Mrs Lockett had already phoned, but I would look after Commodore while Phil went in to see.

In the loose box I unsaddled Commodore and ran my hand over his legs. To my experienced touch there didn't seem to be anything seriously wrong, but he was still trembling a lot and his shoulders were bleeding.

At last Mary came out of the house.

'Tom's in bed,' she said, 'and he says he only needs some sleep, but Mother's sent for the doctor. Gosh, I hope he isn't concussed! What on earth shall we do if he can't ride?'

'Well, what can we do?' I asked. 'Get somebody else?'

'There's nobody else who's any good. We should either have to scratch from the Show, or get some- body else who's no good and ruin the whole team. Blast!'

Mrs Place then came out of the kitchen and said, 'The lunch is ready, so those of you who are still alive had better come and eat it or I'll never get done. All this silly riding! I knew somebody would be breaking their neck.'

Mary pointed out coldly that nobody had broken their neck.

When the vet arrived some of us went in and had lunch, and by then the doctor had come to see Tom.

'I expect you're worried about your young cousin,' he said as he came downstairs.

'We're not a bit worried about *him*,' said Jane; 'what we're worried about is the Show, and is he going to let our team down?'

The doctor looked a bit taken back, but he said, 'Oh, you needn't worry about that. He'll be quite all right in a day or two. He hasn't got any concussion. How you kids miss the worst I wouldn't know. He's knocked a few bruises up, but that's about all.'

'Well, thank goodness for that,' said Lolly, shovelling carrots into her mouth. 'We were *terribly* worried about the Show,' she added; 'I mean, if anybody falls out now, we've had it.'

The doctor stared at us as if we were a lot of callous subhuman things from Outer Space, and then he went off, and Mrs Lockett burst in and cried, 'Well, that's a relief. Tom's asleep and when he wakes up he won't be much the worse for his adventure. Goodness, I'm hungry. Where on earth is Phil? It's half-past two.'

'He's still out with Commodore and the vet,' said Mary, 'and we daren't ask yet for fear of getting some ghastly news. I mean, Tom's got off all right, but has Commodore?'

'Go and see, do,' said Mrs Lockett, sitting down and reaching for the slightly cold stew. 'I can't bear the suspense.'

We all rushed out, and when we got to Commodore's loose box Phil appeared and said, 'What is this, a herd of elephants? Don't all come crowding in, it's enough to give the poor animal heart failure.'

'Is he all right?' shouted Lolly.

'Yes, he is. Mr Poliphant says he's only had a shock and must not be ridden for twenty-four hours.'

'Coo, my hair's nearly gone white!' said Mary. 'I think we'd better all wrap ourselves up in cotton wool and stay in bed until the Show.'

'Feeble idiot!' said Jane. 'I think we ought to go and find a nice ditch and jump it, just to keep our nerve.'

'Oh, no you don't!' said Mary.

At teatime we were all allowed to go up and see Tom. He was sitting up in bed with a cup of tea and a huge chunk of cake, and he grinned sheepishly when we appeared.

'I say, I do feel a mug,' he said.

'So you jolly well ought,' said Phil. 'You should have seen yourself rolling down that hill!'

'We thought you were dead, and the team had had it,' said Jane.

'I don't really remember what happened,' said Tom, 'but I've got about a million bruises, dark purple ones. They'd take a prize in a modern art competition.'

'What you need is a bit of hard riding,' said Mary brutally.

We all buzzed off, and Tom was up and about next day.

But something happened to plunge me into the squalid darkness of utter gloom.

10 Paper-chasing

'Hurray, the programmes for the Show have come,' cried Mary, fetching in a big envelope.

Everybody shouted, 'Oh let me see!' and there was a lot of furious grabbing.

'If you'd just stand back,' said Phil, 'and let's all look in turn. There's one for Mary and Amanda and me, and one for you three kids.'

Mary had first look at our programme, and then she handed it to me, and Phil said, 'I'll give you three minutes.'

The very first thing I looked at was the entry for the senior jumping, and what I saw made a lump of ice go slithering down my back.

It said:

'*Plum* . . . owned and ridden by Amanda Applewood.'

Now it is one thing to play at leading a double life, but to see it down in print is a very different cup of tea. In every event in which I had entered in that programme it said, '*Plum*, owned and ridden by Amanda Applewood.' And Amanda Applewood wasn't going to ride at all, so it was a LIE in cold print, and I had told it! I was deceiving the public and I was a fraud, and I had just realised it, and I felt awful. Whatever would Mummy say? I couldn't bear to think of it, because I knew! I was actually and in cold blood planning to appear at a Show riding somebody else's pony, and calling myself by somebody else's name that I hadn't any right to. Good gracious, I was being a crook! What could they do to me if they found out?

'What's the matter with you, Jillamanda?' said Mary, as that was the name they had all suddenly started calling me by. It had been invented by Jane and they thought it was rather funny. 'You look thunder-struck.'

'It's nothing,' I mumbled, feeling weird.

'You look as if you'd just done a round with twenty-six faults,' said Mary.

I went upstairs to make my bed, but I felt so low that I even wondered if I ought to write to the Committee and say I was a crook, and then pack my case and run away in the stillness of the night. But I couldn't do a thing like that to the Locketts, and wreck their team, especially when they had been so nice to me lately and I was getting to like them.

We spent the morning on ordinary schooling, and fortunately Plum was so good that I didn't have to try very hard.

When we were all tired, Mrs Lockett made us loosen the ponies' girths and sit down on the ground, and said we'd just run over the aids. Of course we all said we knew the aids backwards, and she said we probably thought we did.

'Come on, people,' she said. 'Let's see some intelligence. Perhaps Jillamanda would deign to come out of her dream and tell us exactly what the diagonal aids are, and how you would apply them.'

I went hot, and muttered something about feeling your left rein and pressing with your right leg, and vice versa, and Mrs Lockett said, 'Well, what's so hard about that to make you look so shot up? Has anybody got anything to add?'

Mary said, 'I suppose you ought to keep on looking in the direction you want to go, and keep the pony's head that way too.'

Mrs Lockett said we weren't very bright on the whole, and she hoped we knew more in practice than we seemed to do in theory, and Jane said for the umpteenth time, 'If Mrs Finch-What's-it asks me anything like that I shall die, I know I shall.'

'So shall I,' said Lolly. 'I shall drop down dead at her feet and stain her horrible boots with my gore.'

'You really are the feeblest crowd,' said Mrs Lockett. 'I don't know why I bother with you.'

'Maternal pride, I suppose,' said Phil.

'*Pride!*' said Mrs Lockett with a hollow laugh. 'I'd take more pride in a few decent hens.'

In the afternoon a nice, quiet ride was taken in order to get Tom and Commodore loosened up again, but I don't think it was really necessary as Commodore was quite wickedly full of oats, and spoiling, and Tom was bursting with suppressed energy and would have galloped if Mrs Lockett hadn't been stern about it.

Nobody was in the mood for the nice, quiet ride in spite of Mrs Lockett telling us repeatedly what a lot of good it was doing us and the ponies, and Mary said to me, 'We must look like the sort of prehistoric riding school they had in about 1920; all we want is side saddles and about fifty yards of black skirts surging around our feet.'

When we got home our wrists ached with holding the ponies in, and Jane said she never wanted to hear the word 'collected' again. Mr Lockett said, 'What's all the fuss?' and Mrs Lockett said, 'I've been teaching them that riding isn't just a matter of letting off your high spirits, so we've been doing a bit of slow-marching for a change and they didn't take to it.'

Mr Lockett said, 'Quite right. Mother knows best.'

We all looked as glum as penguins, as one does when grown-ups make this peculiarly grown-up statement; though actually we knew it was true that when it comes to riding the person who teaches you control is worth a million of the person who just lets you have a good time.

However, at breakfast next morning Lolly suddenly said, 'I know what we jolly well ought to have these hols, and I don't see why we shouldn't have it now, and that's a paper-chase.'

'Oh boy!' shouted Jane. 'Bags I lay the trail.'

'Oh no, you don't!' screamed Lolly. 'I thought of it first, so bags I.'

'Don't be silly, you can't lay a trail, you're too young,' said Tom. 'Bags I.'

'You flipping well won't,' said Jane. 'I got it in first.'

'Oh!' shrieked Lolly. 'Jane's said "flipping", Jane said "flipping", she did, she said "flipping" and we're not allowed to –'

'If you don't shut up –' said Phil. He took an enormous gulp of coffee, and said, 'What do you think about a paper-chase, Mum?'

'Well, there's no harm in it,' said Mrs Lockett, 'so long as you don't behave like idiots.'

'The ponies want letting out a bit after yesterday,' said Mary.

'And I want loosening up a bit,' said Tom. 'I feel like a chunk of old iron, in fact I feel like an old iron bedstead, so *I'll* lay the trail.'

Jane and Lolly began to howl again, but Mrs Lockett said, 'Now pipe down, you two. I think it's a good idea for Tom to lay the trail because then he won't be tempted to break his neck leading the chase. So clear the breakfast things, quick, and get the chores done, and we'll all start tearing paper.'

After we had done the usual sordid jobs, like making beds, tidying, etc. (I think tidying is the silliest grown-up chore, because what's the good of putting useful things away in cupboards and drawers when you only want them out again?), feeding and grooming the ponies, and helping Mrs Place to round up a cold lunch, Tom brought his saddle-bags and we all sat round on the study floor and began to tear paper like mad. Fortunately there were stacks of old newspapers in the attic, only Mary was awful, she kept reading bits out of the papers instead of getting on, and she and Jane had a fight because Mary was reading something about the cinema and Jane grabbed it and tore it across, and Mary said, 'Oh, you fool! Now I shan't know what that film was called,' and Jane said, 'What does it matter? It was about 1976 anyway.'

We tore tons of paper, and squashed it down in the saddle-bags, and tore more and more, and squashed that down as flat as it would go, because you always need more paper on a paper-chase than you'd think, which you had better remember if you are ever organising one.

Mrs Lockett said, 'Now, Tom, you have one hour's start, and do be sensible, and don't lead the chase anywhere silly or where people will break their necks trying to follow, because the idea of this is just a good healthy run not a steeplechase. And if you must cross water, see that it's easy for the younger ones, I don't want people turning up soaked.'

'And there's no prize for the first one home, or anything like that,' put in Mr Lockett. 'So there's nothing to break your necks for, but when you get home there'll be toasted crumpets and strawberry jam for tea, I'll see to that.'

'Gosh!' said Jane. 'I wish I was home already.'

'Oh, you funky-monkey!' gloated Lolly. 'Who wanted to lay the trail?'

'Well, if I had I'd have been home to tea first,' grumbled Jane.

It was a nice sunny day with quite a breeze, and not too hot. We got Tom ready at last and mounted on Commodore, and he said, 'You kids will look a sadder and wiser lot when I've done with you. Just you wait.'

Mrs Lockett looked a bit worried, and said, 'Now, Tom –' but Phil said, 'Don't take any notice of him, Mum, he's only trying to be funny.'

So Tom finally cantered off into the blue, and we waited for one hour – which was deadly because we didn't know what to do and the ponies were impatient after seeing Commodore go off alone – and then it was time to start, and we went off with a few whoops from Phil and a lot of good advice from Mrs Lockett who for once wasn't coming with us.

The first trail of paper was only a few yards from the garden gate, down the lane.

'It's quite obvious he's making for the woods,' said Phil, as the fresh ponies broke into a canter. We didn't much feel like hurrying because it was so quiet along the grass track under the trees with fitful sunshine sparkling through, in fact I could hear Mary giving Jane a short lecture about not looking down at her pony's feet when the judge called her in at the showing class, and Jane said, 'Oh shut up and let's have a bit of peace.'

When we got to the crossroads there seemed to be bits of paper all over the place. We decided to take the right fork for the woods, but the trail died out so we had to come back and go the other way, and we picked it up again.

'He's made for the Common,' said Phil. 'We'd better hot it up and gallop.'

We went swooping over the turfy common, it was wonderful, and very easy to follow the trail, only we bigger ones got rather far ahead and then had to wait for Jane and Lolly who grumbled like mad.

Further on, Tom deliberately foxed us by laying a false trail and then doubling back, and we had to scatter and try to pick up the right track. The snag was that we argued about which *was* the right track. Phil and I settled on one, and the other three were equally sure it was another; Mary said the majority ought to decide, so Phil and I gave in and we jogged along a dirty lane with ruts, and I said, 'If Tom came down here he's crazy.'

Phil said, 'I bet he's struck up Donkey Hill, let's risk it,' so we climbed and suddenly found the trail. It was a stiff climb and the ponies began to pant rather dramatically, but we were soon at the top and streaming away down the other side till we struck a main road.

The trail reappeared at a gate opposite, so we went through and found ourselves on some uncultivated land full of rabbit warrens, which slowed us up, in fact Jane came down twice and was told off by Phil, who the next minute was himself sitting down with a thud as Opal side-stepped suddenly while he was off balance.

We decided we didn't think much of Tom's trail-laying.

'He's crackers,' said Mary. 'Why on earth didn't he make for the woods where we'd have had a lovely ride, and then over the hunting country for a few jumps?'

However, Tom hadn't finished with us yet. He took us round an enormous circle and then brought us back nearly to where we started.

'Blow me down!' said Phil. 'He's making for the woods *now*!'

We big ones were still keen, but Jane and Lolly had had nearly enough and were getting fed up. We cantered on enthusiastically, and they dragged behind, and by the time we got to what Phil called the hunting country, and came to fences which had to be jumped, they were in trouble. Nice Weather made a mess of an easy brook, came down with all four feet in the water and a terrific splash, and Jane shrieked and flung her arms round her pony's neck.

'Don't be silly,' said Mary, rapidly dismounting, while we all stopped. 'Come on, Jane, get hold of the reins, do.' She began to haul Nice Weather out, and Jane grumbled, 'I'm soaked to the knees.'

'Well, ride a bit faster and let the wind dry you,' said Mary callously.

At the next fence Lolly's pony flatly refused to do anything. I went back to see if I could help her, but Lolly said she had had enough.

'Come on, Jill,' she said, 'let's go home and get at those crumpets. If we don't I shall be last and there won't be any left.'

I said it was a point of honour never to give up on a paper-chase till you'd followed the trail to its logical conclusion, and Jane who had now joined Lolly and me said there wasn't anything logical about this trail, and were we supposed to be enjoying ourselves or were we not? Because if we were, her idea of enjoyment was to chuck it now and make for the crumpets.

The two younger ones both looked rather a mess and were slumped on their ponies like sacks of potatoes, so I said, 'All right, go on home, we shan't be long,' and galloped after the others.

I caught them up on a steep bank, and there we stopped and looked over miles and miles of country, very toy-like with little fields and farms and tiny church towers, and a village that looked the sort you'd make on the table out of plasticine, and a river that was like a long thread of silver foil. The only thing that was big was the sky. It was lovely, and worth coming for.

'We've jolly well lost the trail altogether now,' said Phil. 'I couldn't care less. It's been fun.'

'I think all the training we've done for this Show on Saturday has been fun,' said Mary, 'and we've learnt a lot. I think it was awfully decent of you to come and help us, Jillamanda, and you're much nicer than they told us you were, so that's that.'

'Hear, hear, clap, clap,' said Phil.

I couldn't say a word. My spirits went down with an awful flop, I could nearly hear them bumping, like dropping a saddle down the stairs.

I tried to tell myself that it couldn't matter now. Only one more day and then the Show, and then it would be over and I would go home. But I would never see the Locketts any more, and we had had such gorgeous times together, and could have been such friends.

We rode home quickly, the breeze in our hair and a lovely feeling of effortless flying, and soon we were putting the ponies in, unsaddling and rubbing down, and then came that gorgeous feeling of being tired and hungry and full of fresh air, and flopping down on the sofa in the dining-room with a piping hot buttered crumpet in one hand and a beaker full of nice boiling drink in the other, and all talking at once.

Tom thought he had been very clever to mislead us so, until Jane and Lolly got him on the carpet and sat on his head till he was nearly smothered, and Mrs Lockett finally called them off.

'Only one more day, and then it's Saturday and the Show,' said Mrs Lockett. 'I don't know what you'd all care to do tomorrow, but I suggest you should each work at the thing that you're weakest at. You ought to know.'

Jane said she was going to practise being called in and not look down at Nice Weather's feet, and Lolly said she was going to do back-reining all day, and Tom said he was just going to try and achieve an air of general smartness, and Mary said she'd mug up a bit more about the horse in sickness and in health in case she got stuck with Mrs Finch-What's-it's questions, and Phil and I decided we'd have a gentle slosh at everything we might be called upon to do. (I mean, just before a Show you either know your stuff or you don't and if you don't it's no good trying to learn anything then. It only puts you in a flap.) So that's what we did the following day.

11   The Show begins

The idea was that we should all get to bed early the night before the Show. If Mrs Lockett said once, 'You must all get to bed early tonight,' she said it a million times, and we heartily agreed; but when the night in question actually came everybody was saying, 'Where's my this, that and the other, if I don't find it tonight I'll never find it tomorrow,' and you can imagine what it was like with five other people all carrying on like that!

Phil didn't do a thing. He just sat there and said, 'I think you people are crazy. What's the good of deciding what you're going to wear now, when you don't know what the weather's going to be like tomorrow?'

Mary gave a yelp, and said, 'Well, we've got to wear shirts, haven't we, whatever the weather is, and that's what we're ironing, yours and Tom's too, you lazy so-and-so!'

Lolly said, 'If we've got to wear macs I'll die. I'll just drop down dead,'

'I don't care,' said Jane. 'My white mac's jolly nice.'

'Oh, you selfish pig!' screamed Lolly. 'Just because you've got a nice mac you don't care if the poor ponies are floundering about in bogs of mud.'

'I didn't say that—' Jane began, but Lolly who was very overexcited just yelled, 'Yes you did, yes you did!' until Mrs Lockett sent her straight up to bed. But she didn't go to bed, she sat on the floor on the landing and kept looking down through the banisters, thinking she was missing something, and Mr Lockett said, 'My gosh! Gymkhanas! If I had my way I'd abolish the lot.'

Then Mary and Jane had a row over a blue shirt which they both said belonged to them, and Phil said, if he had his way he'd abolish girls never mind gymkhanas, and Mary said, 'Just for that I shan't iron your white shirt and you'll have to wear the one with the green splosh on the collar, and I hope you lose marks for a dirty appearance.'

So you can tell we were very worked up.

By the time the shirts were ironed, Jane couldn't find her jodhpur boots, and oh what a fuss! In the end we were all shoved upstairs, and Mary set three alarm clocks for six o'clock because she couldn't trust only one.

I felt a bit weird and cold inside as I climbed into bed with the darkness all around me. It wasn't a nice feeling, and I thought I never wanted to see a Perfect Pony again as long as I lived; and if I could only get through tomorrow without anything awful happening and get home, I'd never go away again, and I never wanted to have any more adventures.

I thought I wouldn't be able to go to sleep, but I did and it seemed only five minutes before Jane came bursting into my room.

'Come on,' she said. 'This is it.'

'Is what?' I said crossly.

'Came the dawn,' she said.

It had come all right! I struggled up in bed, and said, 'What's the time?'

'It's ten to six. We didn't even wait for the beastly

alarm clocks. Mary's gone down to make cocoa for us, and then we'll get cracking on the ponies.'

'What's the weather like?' I shouted, jumping out and rushing to the window.

It was chilly, but dry, and misty in a hopeful sort of way. Goodness knows, I have had a lifetime of experience in gazing at the weather in the dawn of gymkhana mornings, but I did feel a bit dim on this particular one, and quite honestly I don't think I should have minded if there had been an earthquake, a volcano, and four tornados all going on at the same time, so that the Show would be off – which was rather feeble of me, but that's how I felt.

I put on some shorts and a sweater and tore downstairs. Mary shoved a mug of cocoa into my hand. 'Go on,' she said. 'Scoot out there and get weaving.'

The boys were already at work. Automatically I fed Plum and left her with her feed and her water while I dashed about collecting the grooming tools. By now Lolly was doing Gelert's hoofs and was under everybody's feet at the same time, and I was washing Plum's tail, and Phil was yelling, 'Anybody got any more soap flakes?'

Tom said, 'Gosh, Jane's swiped the lot! Just look at that thick soapy water, you could walk on it!'

Jane said she'd finished in any case, and Tom could use the same water, and Tom said, 'I like that! I'm not used to washing Commodore's tail in other people's dirty water.'

We rubbed and brushed and polished, and the morning grew brighter. There was a pink glow in the eastern sky which meant it really was going to be a lovely day.

By the time I was packing up the grooming kit to take with me, and remembering to put in a few lumps of sugar for rewards for Plum (in case she did anything to get rewarded for, which I thought was doubtful), the sun was shining, and Mary was shouting to Phil, 'Pack my grooming tools, will you? I'd better take up a cup of tea to the aged parents.'

'I beg your pardon!' said Mrs Lockett, coming out of the house fully dressed.

By now you could smell breakfast sizzling, and we all dashed in, starving hungry, and fell upon the sausages like wolves.

'Everybody in good heart?' said Mr Lockett.

'You've said it,' said Phil, and I thought, That's funny really, because actually and though they don't know it, *I'm* not really in good heart at all!

However, there wasn't much time to think about hearts. By now everybody was hunting for *something*. You know what it's like on Show mornings? You think you've got everything, and it's always the vital thing that's missing. Jane's jodhpur boots still hadn't turned up, and she was frantic. I found my decent tie, which I thought was lying in a drawer, all creased on the wardrobe floor. All the hats were mixed up. Mary, who had finally got possession of the good blue shirt, found that she couldn't button it and it really was Jane's after all, so Mary had to wear the yellow one which annoyed her as she said yellow was always unlucky for her, and Tom found some paint on the leg of his jodhpurs and didn't know how it had got there.

Poor Mrs Lockett was bawling everybody out and trying to put things right at the same time. She found Jane's boots under the stairs, and they hadn't even been cleaned from last time they were worn, and Jane had the shoe brush in one hand and the boots in the other and put her hand up to brush her hair back and got brown polish all over her nose.

Anyway, you have doubtless lived through similar sordid scenes in your own happy homes, especially if there are several of you in the same family.

To make a long story short, we finally did set off in a cavalcade, and very nice we looked. Six beautiful ponies and six gallant riders, and Mrs Lockett bringing up the rear on her lovely mare, which makes seven, doesn't it? It wasn't far to go, so we all arrived cool and clean. It was a lovely show ground, and everything shone from the fresh paint to the bright green grass, but of course the only thing we were interested in that morning was the hunter competition.

As soon as we rode in we met a girl whom the Locketts knew, who said in a ghoulish voice, 'The course is frightful.'

'Well, what do you expect?' said Mary in a bored superior way. 'It can't be worse than one gets when hunting, or even on a cross-country ride,' and Phil said, 'Good for you, old girl!' and the moaning one looked suitably squashed.

We then went and got our numbers, and mine was 33 which gave me a faint ray of hope, as a double number like that is usually lucky for me, and I once did frightfully well when my number was 22. We joined the other competitors, and they all looked much better mounted and so much more competent and confident than we did, which is something one always feels in competitions, though it is very putting-off.

Then we had a jolly good look at the course, and our hearts went down plonkety-plonk.

There were eight jumps and five of them were fences, with or without brush. Two of them had water on the take-off side, and the worst of all, at the bottom of the hill, had a ditch on the landing side. To our nervous eyes it looked yards across.

Jane said, 'I wish we'd managed to get a bit more of this sort of practice!'

Mary said she felt in her bones that the uphill jumps were going to be her doom. There was also a stream that had to be jumped twice, and a big tree trunk such as you'd find out hunting.

The great moment approached, and the steward called us into the collecting ring and began to explain the course. It all sounded very easy if one knew how, and we stood round shaking and trying not to show it, all except Phil who adored this sort of competition in any case.

A team called Meadrow Riding School went first, three boys and three girls. They were all very well dressed, in identical fawn jodhpurs, white shirts, and green ties. Jane thought they looked professional, but their performance wasn't all that it might have been. Two of them crashed fences with the forelegs, three of them went into the brook instead of across it, and one of them messed up an uphill fence so much that it took several minutes to re-erect it. The two biggest ones, a boy and girl, got clear rounds, but they took so long over them that they had a time disqualification. Altogether the team picked up about twenty-four faults between them.

Then the Rectory team went in, and Janet Hare, the girl we were all afraid of, rode first and did the most perfect clear round I ever saw in my life. All her friends and supporters clapped like mad, and so did we too as it was such a good performance, and Phil said, 'Well, now we know what we're up against!'

Jane said, 'We might as well pack up so far as this event's concerned,' and I said, 'Don't be a feeble idiot,' though I wasn't feeling so encouraged myself, what with wishing I wasn't riding under false pretences and not being too sure how Plum was going to react. My mood wasn't helped either by a weird-looking man who walked by, looked at me and Plum, and muttered, 'That pony's too long in the stride for this job, that's what's the matter with it.'

This was quite untrue, and as Mary pointed out, the man was probably and had momentarily escaped from his keeper, but all the same it didn't cheer me up.

Meanwhile the Rectory team were plodding along, some of them fetching bits of brush down and staggering through the water, but none of them doing too badly, and one other besides Janet Hare did a clear round inside the time limit. In the end they had only clocked up nineteen faults between them and gained twenty points for the two clear rounds.

Our team was riding next but one, and Mary said to me, 'I can't stand much more of this, let's go and get some nourishment,' so we went and had an ice in the marquee, though the others said they would rather stay and watch the opposition. Mary was very confident, and said she didn't see why she and I and Phil shouldn't get clear rounds. We had all done plenty of cross-country riding, and she and Phil had hunted last winter and kept up better than a lot of the grown-ups. She asked, did I hunt Plum at all? and I replied with the perfect truth, no, I didn't, and felt very uncomfortable when she said how surprised she was.

'Well, that makes you a doubtful quantity,' she said, 'and I must say I take a dim view of Lolly. She could easily knock up forty faults on that course.'

'Oh, well, don't let's meet it,' I said, trying to sound carefree, and scooping up the last of my ice which was the watery kind that tastes of synthetic egg.

When we got back to the course, the team that was in was just finishing, in fact we were in time to see the last rider take a lovely toss at an uphill fence.

'Council of war,' said Phil, 'if you two characters have done stuffing yourselves. I'm riding first and I hope I'll set you a good example. Don't any of you gallop, it's too risky, and on the other hand don't try a collected canter between the fences or you won't get anywhere in the time. The thing is a decent hunting pace.'

Lolly said blankly, 'What's a decent hunting pace when it's at home?' and Phil looked at her and said, 'Give me strength! Just *ride*, child, as fast as you can without losing complete control.'

'Gelert knows he isn't really hunting,' said Lolly calmly, 'so I'll have an awful job to make him hurry.'

'Come on,' said Mrs Lockett. 'While you've been talking that team have finished and they've got no clear round and fifteen faults. Ready, Phil?'

Phil looked very nice and competent up there on Opal, and when the bell rang he rode a circle – Opal was bright-eyed and swinging her tail – and went straight and true for the first fence. What happened I can't imagine, but to our horror Opal refused. After that she woke up and took the fence neatly, but we could feel that Phil was put off; however he began to use his legs energetically, and we saw him clear the next two jumps and disappear into the distance below the hill. There was a rather breath-holding few minutes while he was out of sight, wondering what was happening to him down there, but when he emerged riding strongly we were pretty sure that he had done well and lost no time at the stream. Apart from that first unfortunate refusal he had a clear round, and looked very glum about it.

'Just one of those things,' he said, shrugging. 'Go on, Jane, you next.'

Jane appeared to be going off too eagerly.

'I'm going to shut my eyes,' said Mary. 'I can't bear it.'

Jane did an enormous jump at the first fence where it wasn't necessary, and a feeble one at the water jump, but to our amazement she landed over. By the time we lost sight of her she had no faults, but Phil said, 'I hate to think what's happening to her down at the stream. If she's plastered with mud when she reappears we'll know the worst.'

But Jane wasn't even damp. Along she came, with Nice Weather as cool as an ice cream soda and as happy as could be, prancing up the hill and nearly grinning as he approached the uphill fences. Jane used her stick, Nice Weather seemed to be pulling and I for one shut my eyes. When I opened them again there was Jane miraculously over the first and her pony straightening out beautifully for the last jump, and taking it in fine style.

'Clear round,' said the loudspeaker.

'Blimey, if I didn't have luck!' panted Jane, tumbling off her pony at our feet. 'Every single thing went right. I ought to have had about ten faults, and I don't know how on earth we did the water jumps, but Nice Weather didn't even get his feet wet. It was wonderful!'

We were speechless as we thumped Jane on the back, it was so unexpected, but then riding always is, that's part of the beauty of it.

Tom went next. He seemed to have trouble with

his timing and rode too carefully, then he seemed to realise he was losing time and took the next jump much too fast. Crash! Down came the rails and we groaned. Tom sped on towards the ditch, but there also Commodore came unstuck. They finished the course without any more bad mistakes, but managed to collect six faults.

'Sorry,' he said, coming back. 'I rode like a clot.' I think we all felt sympathetic.

''Sme now,' said Lolly. 'Let's see if I can knock spots off Jane.'

'I can't bear to watch this,' said Mary.

However Lolly had her pony well collected, and did all the right things, and the crowd liked her very much as they always do like anybody who's only about ten, if they ride well. She got a clap each time she cleared a jump and you could tell it was doing her good. She was rather a long time out of sight in the bottom, and when she reappeared she had obviously been in the water, in fact it was dripping off her hat and Gelert was soaking, but she got over the uphill fence and the last jump and there she was, still smiling, with only four faults.

Mary let out her breath, which she had literally been holding all the time, and we all said, 'Jolly good show.'

It was my turn now. All I cared about was not letting the side down. I tried to pretend I was riding at Chatton on my own pony, and how happy and confident I should be if I were! For one thing I did bless Plum, her timing was so good and she knew what she had to do, so that we were over the first jump almost before I realised it. After that I got hold of the situation myself.

I patted Plum gently between the ears, and we came

to the jump with water on the take-off side. I felt her go up just a fraction of a second too soon and some gorse flew, and at the ditch in the bottom she unfortunately went in with her hind legs. I got her round and up the hill, but I had by now realised that she was not what you'd call a hunting type of pony, and I heard her heels clip sharply on the rail of the uphill jump. Nothing awful happened to us, though by now I wasn't exactly sure what we had totted up. I thought it was four faults and Mary thought it was only two, but it turned out to be four.

There was only Mary to ride now, and she simply had to do a clear round if we weren't going to have the Rectory team miles ahead of us.

To our terrific delight she did it. She had probably never ridden better in her life, and she had luck too. We finished the competition with two faults less than the Rectory team, so won the points plus Lolly's bonus. It was a magnificent start, and we went off to lunch feeling we had been more lucky than we had ever dreamed of.

12   Rosettes and a shock

We unsaddled the ponies, put on their halters, and left them under the trees in the long soft grass to have a rest.

We settled down to our lunch in a comfortable corner behind the horse boxes, and I must say Mrs Lockett had the right ideas about picnic food. When I was a kid I once went for a picnic with my cousin Cecilia – about whom you have most certainly read in my previous books – and her mother, and the food was depressing; slices of cold beef and the sort of rolls that are soft outside and hard inside when they ought to be the other way round, and not enough butter, and orangeade that had gone warm, and jam tarts that had slightly melted and stuck to your face when they weren't falling flat on the ground jam side down.

Well, Mrs Lockett's lunch consisted of super sandwiches, not just the potted meat kind but the mashed salmon kind with lettuce and tomato in, and the bread was lovely and new. Then there were cold chipolatas on sticks, very well browned, and crisp rolls and heaps of butter, and very plummy fruit cake, and to drink we had cans of Coke from the fridge in the refreshment tent, and we finished up with some gorgeous-tasting apples and a bar of nut-milk chocolate each. If you think I am a pig I am very sorry, but I can't help dwelling upon this glorious feast, though Mummy may put a pencil through this page if she sees it before it gets into print.

Mrs Lockett hurried us along as she began to collect the debris, which I need hardly say we put carefully into a bag to take home and burn, as I expect you always do, or else you aren't the right sort of horsy person to have picnics at all.

'Now get along, everybody,' she said, 'and spruce up the ponies, and perhaps you boys will help Lolly with Gelert, as he was the only one that got wet.'

'Well, don't rub it in,' protested Lolly. 'I only got four faults and you got a jolly good bonus on me when we won the event.'

The first event of the afternoon was the under-fourteen showing class, which included Jane and Lolly, to say nothing of Tom who, still in the age group, felt rather large and elderly and said, 'I jolly well wish I hadn't entered with all these kids.'

'Never mind the kids,' said Mrs Lockett. 'Just show your pony!'

We all went along to get them ready and mounted, hair combed, ties straight, on speckless ponies, and they really did look very nice. Their jodhs were well pressed and their shirts well ironed, and Tom and Lolly stuck to their velvet crash caps while Jane insisted on wearing her beloved bowler a bit too far back on her head.

'There go our hopes!' said Mary with satisfaction as they rode off, the ponies' tails swishing sweetly, and Mrs Lockett's last minute instructions about, 'Look straight in front of you . . . keep your heels down . . . don't crowd the pony in front . . . if you're asked a question, don't mumble, sound as if you knew . . . look alert, not half-dead,' ringing in the kids' ears.

At last they all got into the collecting ring, and a

very big entry it was, forty-seven. They started riding round. Some of those kids looked awfully good, and on the other hand – as it always is at shows – some of them looked as if they had never been on a pony before. Some of the kids had been all dolled up by their mothers in hunting kit even with violets in their buttonholes, and others looked as if they needed a bath and their shirts washing; some rode round looking as if they'd spent their whole lives collecting prizes, while others looked so hopeless you couldn't help being sorry for the poor little miseries. And some of them were just plain good!

We kept our eyes firmly fixed on our three entries.

'Jane, for goodness' sake, keep your hands down!' breathed Mary in anguish. She said to me, 'She always gets her hands up when she's nervous, the idiot.'

'Oh gosh!' muttered Phil. 'Commodore's too fresh, he's side-stepping all the time and Tom's getting rattled.'

'Lolly's OK,' I said.

'She's too stiff,' sighed Mary. 'She's trying too hard.'

'I bet you anything that Furze child's called in first,' said Phil. 'She makes you sick, she's so good.'

'If she's the best she deserves to win,' said Mrs Lockett sharply. 'For pity's sake, don't forget to be sporting.'

'What team does she belong to?' I asked, and Mary said, 'It's a team called Pleasance Farm, and actually she's the only one who's any good in it, so even if she wins it won't do us much harm in the final results.'

'There you are!' shouted Phil. 'She's called in first.'

'Oh, come on, Jane! Come on, Tom! Come on, Lolly!' I breathed.

They were still riding round in the lovely sunshine,

over the beautiful green turf, and now they were cantering, and at the bend Jane was on the wrong leg and we all let out a groan. Then a boy was called in second and a very thin girl of about fourteen on a flea-bitten grey was third, and another very small boy fourth.

'I can't bear it,' said Phil. 'Take me home, somebody.'

Tom was fifth, but Jane and Lolly were nowhere, on the second row.

'Perhaps they'll reverse the placings,' I said hopefully. 'They often do. Perhaps Tom will get moved up.'

The children were now leading out in hand, and unsaddling, and being spoken to by the judge, who *wasn't* Mrs Wattington-Finch after all; but alas, all the replacing that happened was that the second and third changed over. The rosettes were given out, the rabble rode off, the winners galloped round the ring, and we had to face it. Not one of our three had got a place! It was too frightful.

When we joined them they looked as blue as blue.

'Ghastly!' said Tom. 'Murder! Commodore behaved like a rocking horse.'

'Jane, you were on the wrong leg,' said Mary.

'I wouldn't be surprised if I was on four wrong legs,' said Jane, full of gloom. 'I was nervous, and I've never been before.'

Lolly said, 'It was that beastly judge, Colonel Salmon. He never did like me. He always ignores me.'

'Please don't let's have any inquests,' said Mrs Lockett briskly. 'You were none of you good enough, and that's the bottom of it. And what you say is sheer nonsense, Lolly, and we won't have any of that sort of talk in *our* team, please! We've got no marks in that competition, that's what it amounts to, so now pull yourselves together and make up your minds that you're going to do a lot better. I've seen all three of you ride like winners, so you *can* do it, you just made mistakes. Forget 'em now, and carry on.'

'So it's up to us big ones!' said Mary. 'It's our showing class next, so come on, comrades, and good luck to the lot of us. We'll need it.'

Phil and Mary and I got ready. I was scared stiff, I can tell you! What with worrying about pretending not to be myself but somebody else, and the responsibility of making up for what the younger ones hadn't done, and a pony who was supposed to be perfect but which I had never ridden in a showing class before, I was nearly round the bend, and I had got to do well!

I must say, Plum looked superb. She shone and gleamed, her mane and tail were like floss silk, her eyes were bright yet kind and steady, and she held her head beautifully. I couldn't help wishing she wasn't called by that sordid name, Plum. In fact I couldn't think of a name noble enough for her, though if she had been mine I bet I would have done.

We all went into the ring, and there were thirty-nine of us. I tried just to think what a wonderful sight it was, all those riders, and how lucky I was to be riding and to have a super pony like Plum to ride on. We began to circle the ring, and it comforted me to see how well Plum was holding her head and how smooth her pace was. She was confident if I wasn't, and that pulled me up with a jerk; I mean, you mustn't ever allow your own feelings to let your pony down.

We trotted and cantered at the judge's orders. In front of me was a boy on a wild-eyed bay which he could hardly hold in. I was terrified that before long we should collide and never be able to disentangle. I just held back and hoped for the best. I couldn't see anything of Phil or Mary, and I daren't look even out of the corner of my eye. Somebody's pony ran backwards and messed up three others, and I did hope that none of our team were involved. I tried hard to do everything right. Suddenly I became conscious of a voice behind me saying, 'Go on, it's you!' I barely took this in; then another voice floated to me on the breeze, 'Go on in! You're 33, aren't you?' I pulled myself together. I had been called in, and called in first!

I rode in in a daze, and a minute later there was somebody on my right side. It was Phil! I gave him a sort of nervous half-grin, and then we both sat gazing straight in front between our ponies' ears. Someone rode into third place on the other side of Phil. I sneaked a flashing glance. Gosh! Crumbs! It was Mary! The three of us, in first, second and third places! It was like a dream, I thought I must be going mad, I even lost the rein and grabbed a handful of Plum's mane, and the judge looked at me as if he thought I was swooning with the heat.

He looked rather a nice judge, rather like an elderly tortoise in a hairy suit, and he had a frightfully just expression.

He patted Plum and said, 'That's a lovely pony you've got, my dear,' and I felt a guilty pang as I always did when anybody referred to Plum as 'my' pony. He then told me to do a figure of eight, which was just up Plum's street, she did a lovely one and we came back into line. Phil was told to walk out, collect and trot which he did without a fault, and Mary was apparently told to do anything she liked because she did an extended walk and a few rather good half-passes. Then we had to unsaddle. By now

I was in the state of mind when I shouldn't have been surprised to see that Plum had broken out into millions of harness galls, but of course she was all right, and the judge peeped into her ears and was I glad I'd done them thoroughly!

Phil and Mary were also okayed, and the next minute the rosettes were being handed out, red for me, blue for Phil and yellow for Mary, and we were galloping round the field looking as cool as we could and wanting to scream hip-hip-hooray. It was amazing.

As I rode out through the gate I heard somebody's voice say plaintively, 'I should have won that competition easily if Globetrotter hadn't fouled a fetlock over that beastly fence this morning,' and I thought smugly, That's what you think, whoever you are!

Mrs Lockett was waiting for us. 'Not bad, not bad at all,' she said, meaning, 'How terrifically good.'

'I can't believe it,' said Mary, slithering down off Agate and fanning herself with her hat. 'Jillamanda, you were *very* hot, and Plum looked so gorgeous she must have blinded the judge with her beauty. Just imagine, all three of us! That's a lovely bunch of marks.'

Tom came bounding up. 'I've just heard,' he gasped. 'Congrats, all of you. And what do you think I've been doing while you were away?'

'Guzzling, I expect,' said Phil coldly.

'I won the bending,' said Tom, and added, 'You beast!'

'You didn't!'

'It was on the gymkhana field,' said Tom, 'Over there. And Jane and Lolly are there now, doing the under-fourteen Musical Mats.'

'Why on earth didn't you stop and watch them?'

asked Mary, and Tom said, 'I wanted an ice cream, but they were both still in when I left.'

'Come on, let's go,' said Mary, and she and Phil and I ran off, just arriving at the gymkhana field as the competition ended.

Lolly came rushing towards us with her face scarlet, her tie under her ear, and her cap on the back of her head.

'I'm second!' she screamed, waving her blue rosette. 'And I was the youngest in it, except for the Baines kid. And Jane fell plonk on her nose or she'd probably have been third.'

Jane came up looking a bit crushed, and we told her about our success in the showing class, which she wouldn't believe until we showed her the rosettes.

'I'm jolly glad,' she said, 'But it's time I did something. I've mucked everything up so far.'

'You'll probably win the Gretna Green with me,' said Lolly, and added rashly, 'if you can't pull anything off by yourself.'

Of course Jane went for her, and the next minute they were fighting like mad, just like they did in the stable yard at home, and not having any dandy brushes handy they started bashing each other with their hats, and a very dressed-up woman who was going by said to the man she was with, 'That settles it, Mirabelle doesn't get a pony. It turns children into hooligans.'

I felt so sorry for Mirabelle and for the wrong view of horsemanship that Jane and Lolly had started in the breast of Mirabelle's misguided mother that I could have murdered the two of them, and when Phil and Mary had got them apart I told them what I had heard, and to do them credit they were upset about it, because of course they had been taught that whatever you do you must never do anything to bring discredit upon the noble cause of equitation.

'Well, never mind,' said Lolly cheering up at last. 'I expect Mirabelle will get a pony in the end if she goes on and on at her mother long enough.'

Jane said, 'What's the next competition anyway?'

It was the team race, and there were eleven teams riding, so that meant three heats of three and one of two teams. We were riding in the third heat. We had arranged for Phil to ride first, to try and get a bit of a lead; then Mary to try and increase the lead; then Lolly because we knew she wouldn't wait any longer without getting too excited and doing something silly. After Lolly would be Tom to make up anything Lolly had lost, and then Jane and finally me.

The three teams lined up, and off we went. Unfortunately Phil didn't get any lead at all, he and his opponent dead-heated. Mary took the stick a bit quicker than the other girl, and gained a lead of about half a length. We were all terrified that Lolly would drop the stick, as she was waiting for it with her tongue hanging out and her eyes sticking out, but she got it and was away, though she lost the lead that Mary had gained and dead-heated with the rider on her left. Tom got off to a good start, but Commodore stumbled and both opponents shot ahead, however, one of them stumbled too, and Tom came home like a rocket, fairly flinging the stick at Jane. Jane got Nice Weather into the maddest gallop you ever saw and made up the gap; she pushed the stick at me, and just at that minute Nice Weather crowded Plum who side-stepped and both opponents whizzed away in front of me.

'Come on, Plum!' I shouted, my knees rammed close, crouching down like a jockey, gathering in the short rein. She rose to the occasion like a champion and for about the first time in my life I knew what the books meant when they said, 'He rode like the wind.' Gosh, I think it must have been like riding in the Derby! Plum flew, her hoofs barely touched the ground. We were level with the other two, passing them, and home by half a head.

The other five yelled as I tumbled down into their midst.

'Jolly good, jolly good!'

'It was Plum,' I said, breathless. 'She was super-sonic.'

So we won our heat, and soon we had to ride in the final with three other teams. In the end the Rectory team just beat us, but we got bonus marks for Lolly being under ten.

The next event was the under-fourteen obstacle race.

'When I was a kid,' said Phil, sounding about a hundred years old, 'I used to do this. Honestly, it puts years on you.'

However, Jane and Lolly weren't daunted, and Jane said, 'I'll win this if I lose all my fingernails and burst into flames, as I haven't won anything yet,' and an old lady who was passing said, 'Listen to that poor child. Do they really lose their fingernails and catch fire? It shouldn't be allowed.' And the girl she was with said, 'Good gracious, no, Granny, you must have been brought up in the ark,' and the Granny said, 'Well, I used to play a very wicked game of croquet, very wicked. I once broke my uncle's ankle.'

Tom began to giggle and the girl with the granny glared at him, and after that we started calling him the Ankle's Uncle.

The obstacle race was just about the biggest chaos

you ever dreamed of. There was everything in it.
The juniors had to crawl through drain-pipes, dress
up in old-time clothes miles too big for them, ride
backwards in the saddle, walk their ponies blindfold
between bottles, eat dry biscuits, and whistle John
Peel. Everybody was roaring with laughter, and Jane
was inspired. She was streets ahead of everybody else,
you'd think she'd been brought up on obstacle races
since she was about two. Anyway, she won all right
and was she thrilled! Lolly was last, because she was
wallowing about in a sort of Victorian nightdress and
got it over her head and wandered right off the course,
and then Gelert saw the gate and made for it, and
the next thing Lolly knew she was being carried by
Gelert into the paddock, and when she got back the
race was over.

'Who won?' she said.

'Well, you didn't,' said Phil.

'I did,' said Jane.

'Go on,' said Lolly. 'I don't believe you. You never
win anything.'

Mary and I looked at each other, and in a second
she had grabbed Jane and I had grabbed Lolly or
there would certainly have been another fight, and
Jane showed her red rosette and Lolly was made to
apologise.

We big ones next went in for Musical Mats for
the seniors, and I managed to come in first. Plum
was very good at it, very quick, and able to stop
dead when the music did and swerve in without
prompting. She had evidently had lots of practice
with the real Amanda. A boy from the Bolt Farm
team was in with me at the end, and I just beat him
to it by running a spot faster. Tom to his delight
was third.

He and Lolly were also second in the Gretna Green with none of the rest of us anywhere.

'And now for tea before the jumping,' said Mary. 'I think we're doing pretty well for marks, aren't we, Mother? I've lost count.'

'Not at all bad,' said Mrs Lockett. 'But don't get pleased with yourselves. Games don't carry many marks, and your score will depend on the jumping, so don't eat too much tea.'

'And I bet it's a gorgeous tea,' said Jane. 'Just my luck.'

We rubbed the ponies down, and tied them in the cool of the trees' shade to have a good rest; and then we went to the competitors' tea tent. The sandwiches and cakes looked super and Jane said, 'Blow the butterflies in my tummy, better to feed them than starve them, anyway.'

Feeling a bit guilty we began on the ham rolls, and then a boy standing near us said, 'Ask for some of those cakes that the Rector's wife made, they're smashing, and don't let Mrs Mead push you off with the ones she made, because the Rector's wife's ones have got tons more nuts in.'

So we did.

At last we'd finished and came laughing out of the tea tent into the sunshine.

'Hello!' cried a voice. 'There you are, Jill. I thought I'd pop along and have a look at you. How are you doing?'

I blinked and nearly fell flat on my face.

It was Amanda Applewood.

13   Happy me

Talk about nearly passing out!

'Hello,' I said in a terrified bleat.

'How's Plum?' said Amanda cheerfully. 'Bearing up?'

'Um – yes,' I croaked, trying to walk on. But Amanda wasn't allowing that.

'Are these the Locketts?' she asked in an interested sort of way, and by now they were staring at her. She looked quite something, in blue slacks, and a bright green anorak, and earrings.

I nodded dumbly, because by now I had given up all hope of the ground opening and swallowing me.

Amanda grinned at Mary. 'Sorry I let you down and all that,' she said. The Locketts all looked at me, as much as to say, 'Who's your friend and is she mad?', especially as Amanda had by now attached herself to us and looked as if she intended to stay for the rest of the proceedings.

'What's up?' she said. 'Anything wrong?'

'We don't know who you are,' said Jane bluntly.

'Gosh!' said Amanda. 'I thought everybody in the world knew who I am. I'm Amanda Applewood, of course. The one that ought to have come and stayed with you only I wangled out of it and Jill came instead.'

I couldn't say a word. I just swallowed.

Mrs Lockett said, 'But –'

It was horrible. I suddenly broke out, 'It's all my fault. I didn't tell you. Amanda ought to have told you on the telephone, and she didn't, and I was mad with her, and I thought I'd pay her out by being her and being beastly to everybody, and I couldn't keep it up, but by then it was too late and I thought you'd send me home, and oh I wish I hadn't come and now it's going to ruin everything –' I choked.

'My Russian rabbits!' said Amanda. 'What a scream!'

Mary said, 'Then you're somebody else! But who – I mean –'

'I let them put Amanda's name in the programme,' I said miserably, 'and I expect it's a crime or something, and I wish I hadn't. And now I've wrecked the team and everything.'

'But who are you?' said Mrs Lockett.

'Jill Crewe,' I muttered.

'Crumbs!' said Lolly. 'Well, I must say, I'm jolly glad you're not Amanda.'

'I'm terribly sorry,' I said. 'Now I've spoilt everything. I suppose I'd better go home.'

'What for?' said Amanda, staring at me.

'Because I can't go on pretending to be you on the programme, now everybody knows,' I said wretchedly.

'Why should you?' said Mrs Lockett. 'It really is the most peculiar muddle, but now we're getting it sorted out I can't see there's much harm done.'

I looked at her in amazement. 'But it says on the printed programme that I'm Amanda Applewood, and I'm not,' I said. 'I've been feeling absolutely awful all the time. Don't I get disqualified?'

'Nonsense,' said Mrs Lockett, 'we can soon put that right. I'll just go over to the Stewards' Tent. What did you say your name was?'

'Jill Crewe,' I mumbled.

'Right. Just wait here.' She walked away, and Amanda began to giggle. 'Coo, you are bright!' she said to me. 'Fancy pretending to be me all the time. How did you keep it up?'

'It was very hard,' I said, 'because I'm not a bit like you.'

I could hardly believe that things were beginning to turn out right, it was like a fairytale.

'Why on earth didn't you tell us before?' said Mary.

'Because I thought you'd be furious and send me home, and I wanted to ride in the team because I liked you.'

'I can understand,' said Phil. 'We liked you too, in fact we couldn't understand why you were so decent when everybody said Amanda Applewood was such a –' he stopped and went rather red.

'Oh, don't mind me!' said Amanda, glaring at him. 'I've no feelings.'

'Don't take any notice of my brother,' said Mary. 'He – er – he's not quite all there, actually.'

'Oh, really?' said Amanda. 'I wondered.' Phil nearly burst.

Just then the loudspeakers gave a sort of gurgle, and the next minute it came out loud and clear, 'There is a small correction to be made in your programmes. Instead of "*Plum*, owned and ridden by Amanda Applewood", kindly read, "*Plum*, owned by Amanda Applewood and ridden by Jill Crewe", throughout. That's all.'

'Well, that's OK,' said Phil.

'Gosh!' I said. 'Is that all?' I simply couldn't believe it, that after all my misery everything was turning out right and it was so simple.

'I don't see that it matters who you are, you can jolly well ride,' said Jane. 'And we'd rather have you than anybody.'

I felt as if nineteen thousand tons of bricks had fallen off my back. Everything was all right, and I wasn't going to be chucked out of the team, and I could go on riding as if nothing had happened. I felt so wonderful I could have jumped a twenty-foot fence. I almost loved Amanda. To think that I had almost swooned with the shock when I saw her appear outside the tea tent, thinking the End Had Come, and yet everything had been so easily put right.

'What do you people do next?' Amanda asked.

'Jumping,' said Lolly. 'Jane and I do the junior jumping, and the others do the senior jumping, and if we're going to win a prize at the end we've simply got to get some placings.'

'Good for you,' said Amanda. 'I hope the opposition fall down at the jumps and break their necks, or have fits, or something.'

We thought this was an unsportsmanlike attitude, but it was Amanda all over.

'I'm dying to have a look at old Plum,' she said, so we strolled over to where the ponies were. 'I say, she looks smashing,' cried Amanda, 'you must have looked after her. I bet she likes you better than me by now.'

'Oh no, she doesn't, she's frightfully glad to see you, in fact she's thrilled,' I said hastily. This was not strictly true, as Plum had just given her rightful owner a completely non-recognising look; but Amanda was satisfied, and slapped Plum's shoulder, and said, 'Buck up, old girl.'

'I say!' said Mary to Amanda, 'I just can't get over you, letting Jill do your dirty work, staying with us.

You must have thought we were a horrible lot if you hated the idea of staying with us.'

'Dirty work!' yelled Amanda. 'I like that. It was only that I wanted to do as I liked in the hols for once instead of being made to do what other people wanted. And Jill's had a whale of a time.'

'Not all the time,' I said. 'Some of the time I was slinking about like a crook.'

Everybody laughed their heads off, and I said, 'It's all right, you can laugh now, but I didn't laugh when I was trying to be Amanda.'

Just then Mrs Lockett came up and said, 'Please come and help with the young ones, they're all in a tizz-wazz over the jumping and Lolly says her boots are too tight, so do you think you could scout round among the people we know, Mary, and borrow her a pair of fives?'

Mary dashed off, and Amanda said, 'I'm looking forward to watching the kids jump. They'll probably beat you big ones into fits.'

'That's all we wanted!' I said gloomily.

We found Tom, Jane, and Lolly standing by their beautifully immaculate ponies looking pale, and Lolly bootless and fussing like anything. However, before she could blow her top Mary dashed up with some borrowed size five boots, and in two ticks they were on Lolly.

'They haven't got the same feel as mine,' Lolly grumbled.

'Oh, don't be so narky!' snapped Jane. 'I don't see how, if your boots fitted you this morning, they've suddenly stopped fitting you this afternoon.'

I think another battle would have been on, but at that very minute the competitors were called into the ring, and we all gasped a few hasty Good Lucks. The large entry rode into the ring and began inspecting the jumps. Our three seemed to our anxious eyes to be taking more interest in the other riders than in the jumps, till Lolly suddenly became very concentrated, marching Gelert up to each fence or wall and fairly pushing his head over.

'She really does try,' said Mary. Then everybody rode out again, and it was time for the first competitor, a very cool-looking girl with a straight back who looked as if she had spent all her life doing jumping competitions much more important than this one.

However, she didn't look so good for very long, as she brought down the wall which was the second jump. There seemed to be a hoodoo on that wall. You have probably noticed in jumping competitions that there is often one jump which the ponies simply hate – for no apparent reason. One pony brings it down, the next refuses, and after that the rot spreads and nobody can take it. It was like that with this wall. After four competitors had messed it up, it became monotonous, and there was a feeling going round that *nobody* could jump this unjumpable wall.

'Looks to me,' said Phil, 'that the first kid who jumps that wall will be quids in.'

'Well, here comes Lolly,' said Mary, 'I hardly dare look.'

Lolly looked both brave and cocky. She sat very straight, and riding up to the brush fence she took off with beautiful timing and soared over with inches to spare.

'Now for it,' said Phil. We all stared till our eyes hurt, anything could have happened to Lolly at that moment. She went straight for the wall, much too fast really, gave her head a little shake, collected Gelert at just the right moment, went up like a bird, and as

Gelert gaily kicked his heels we knew it was all right. They were over and down as light as a dewdrop and the crowd clapped like mad.

'Oh, good old kid!' howled Phil.

Lolly went cleverly on to do a clear round, and being obviously younger than most of the competitors the crowd loved her. She rode out in a gale of clapping.

'I can hardly believe it –' began Mary, but Phil interrupted excitedly, 'Shut up, it's Tom now – look!'

Lolly had broken the hoodoo, and Tom jumped the wall without any faults, and also the next two jumps.

'Oh legs – legs!' breathed Phil as Tom began to bring Commodore round for the tall gate, but alas, only too obviously he was on the wrong one and off balance. He got four faults at that jump and two at the last one, which had rather a wide spread. We felt very sorry for him, because it must be a frightful feeling for a boy of fourteen to be beaten by his sister aged ten.

There were several indifferent rounds, and then another clear one. Then it was Jane. She looked quite happy and her pigtails scarcely swung as she popped over the brush fence. Nice Weather's heels clicked hard on the top of the dreaded wall, but nothing fell.

'What luck!' said Mary. 'Jane does have such luck at that sort of thing; if it's me something always falls.'

With a mixture of luck and skill Jane went on popping over jumps, and approached the last one well on balance but rather shyly.

'Too slow,' said Phil. 'She'll never do it.'

'But she has!' I shrieked. And she had. Honestly, she didn't deserve to because her timing was hardly right, but she was over. A clear round.

Actually there were four clear rounds, and while we

were waiting for the jump-off we all got hold of Jane and Lolly and started to give them advice.

'You can just lay off,' said Lolly. 'If I get any more advice it'll start pouring out of my ears.'

'Advice isn't any good to me,' said Jane. 'I know I got round by sheer luck, and it's evidently my day.'

Four selected jumps were raised six inches, and the four with clear rounds did their stuff, our two and two from the Rectory team. The suspense was nearly unbearable. Lolly rode first and got a clear round; then Cecil Smith from the Rectory team also got a clear round. Jane came next, and she must have been carrying shoals of luck with her, because she did at least three frightful things and got away with them and did a clear round. Then the other girl rode in and took the first three jumps so beautifully that the result seemed assured, until she suddenly clocked up three faults at the triple bar.

They didn't have another jump-off. It meant that our team got two places and the Rectory team one, so with Lolly's bonus we scored a big advantage in points.

'That kid will never let us forget it,' said Tom. 'She'll be impossible to live with after this.'

But we were all so thrilled that when Jane and Lolly came back, having done so magnificently, we carried them off to the refreshment tent and bought them all the ices they could eat, about five each. They were lucky because they didn't have to ride any more.

I felt sorry for Tom because he felt low at having done badly in the jumping while his little sister had done so well.

'Never mind,' he said, 'I've got another chance in the senior, and I'm going to get a place if it kills me.'

14 The last competition

A lot of super-competent-looking people rode into the ring. It was the old, old feeling that everybody else looks better and rides better and has a far better pony than you have – only the last certainly didn't apply on this occasion, as Plum looked gorgeous and had been exciting stares of admiration from other people the whole afternoon. But being a bit on the nervous side I could only say to myself, 'I hope she's going to be as good as she looks.' She certainly felt very steady and her stride was long and free as we went round the jumps, and she popped her head over each one and wrinkled her nose a bit as much as to say, 'Well, that one's OK.' I hoped she was right!

As soon as the actual jumping started it was obvious that the only real opposition we were up against was from the Rectory team. The first to ride was the Rector's son, John Peters, and he didn't seem as if he could care less about having to ride first. This is something which has never fallen to my lot in all my vast experience, and I have always hoped it never will, as it must take terrific character to feel nonchalant – or look it – under such circumstances. John was one of those riders who holds his pony back so tightly between jumps that his canter looks strung up, and the pony jumps from practically a standstill in a nerve-racking way. I'm sure you have seen people like this at Shows, and your heart comes crawling up into your throat watching them, and then when the jump is done it sinks back again like a very cold ice going down. John got two faults, gave his pony two brisk pats, and rode out.

Then a mixed bunch of people rode in turn; some got refusals that put them out of the running, others rode badly and piled up faults, and some just had the sort of bad luck that makes you shiver, thinking it might happen to you. One of these was a girl from the Rectory team. She was doing beautifully and had taken the first four jumps so well that I was sure she was going to get a clear round, then just as she was approaching the fifth a dog fight broke out beside the rails, the pony shied, lost his balance, tried to jump and brought the whole lot down. It was a terrible shame and as the girl rode off the judges glared with annoyance at people who would let their dogs behave like that during a competition, and the crowd said 'Ooooh!' in sympathy.

'Makes you go cold,' murmured Mary. 'Could have been one of us.'

Then came the usual laugh which happens in most jumping competitions when somebody's pony has too much sense of humour and decides he's in the ring for fun, and everything comes down, and the crowd roars with laughter, and the shattered competitor rides out nearly weeping and trying to look as though she doesn't care. I am frightfully sympathetic, as it could happen to me; and if you ever see this happen I hope you will be sympathetic too and not jeer.

Janet Hare of the Rectory team got a most beautiful clear round with pretty and graceful jumping, and we all clapped her when she got back.

I expect you are dying to know how our lot got on – or perhaps by now you couldn't care less, in which case I suggest you give this book to your friend Caroline and go and do your jigsaw puzzle.

Phil was the first of our team to jump. He looked fine and so did Opal, and his take-offs and timing were so competent that the most knowledgeable people clapped every time he was over. And then at the sixth jump – the triple – for no apparent reason Opal gave him three refusals. Whatever gets into ponies' minds that they occasionally do this? It was too disappointing, and we who were watching were terribly sorry for poor Phil.

'Whatever happened?' asked Mrs Lockett as he joined us, very downcast.

'Dunno,' said Phil. 'Just one of those things.' He then grinned very sportingly and said, 'I don't care, if some of the others do well and make up for me.'

Mary was good. She only reaped two faults, and how she managed to get them I don't know. We didn't even see or hear Agate's hoofs touch the top bar of the gate, but they must have done, as it fell. I don't think Mary realised either, because as she rode out and the loudspeaker said, 'Number 47, two faults', she looked up with quite a shocked look on her face. She thought she had done a clear round, and we had to tell her what had happened. Poor old Mary, she was disappointed, and personally I can't think of anything worse.

It was Tom who did the clear round! Tom, who was just fourteen and still in the junior class, where he hadn't even shone. He came out of the ring looking dazed, and muttering, 'It isn't true.'

'Oh, Tom, however did you do it?' gasped Mary, thumping him on the back.

'I didn't,' said Tom. 'I had my eyes shut at every jump.'

'But your timing was so good. I've never seen you take off so well before.'

'Fluke,' said Tom, rubbing his head with amazement. Then he broke out, 'I don't care if I never get a clear round again. I wanted this, and I've done it, and now I'm bound to be in the jump-off and I may get in the first four.'

I may add that by now there were already five clear rounds, and with all my heart I hoped to make it six.

I expect by now you are all gasping with boredom and don't even want to know what happened to me. If so, just turn over a few pages and get on with the story, but if you're still interested, here it comes.

As soon as I was actually riding into the ring I began to feel all right, though slightly dreamlike. Plum was in form and felt even lighter in hand than usual, and as I rode her round waiting for the bell she gave her pretty head one or two cocky little flicks, and then went into her canter perfectly. At the very first jump, the brush fence, when I felt her gather up her legs so carefully and land so lightly my feeling of horror left me, and I put all I'd got into riding this beautiful pony in a way that was worthy of her. My only spot of horror was at the wall when for a minute I felt Plum flinch and knew she didn't like it, but I helped her all I could – and I'll admit it – listened for the crash. It didn't come, and we landed sweetly on the turf and cantered on in one flowing movement.

The three white bars of the final jump sparkled in the sunshine, Plum extended herself beautifully, and the next thing I heard was the roar of the crowd and the loudspeaker singing out, 'Number 33, clear round', the sweetest music in a rider's ears.

Of the six clear rounds, two were ours, and the team were so excited we could hardly speak.

'I'm not giving you any advice,' said Mrs Lockett to Tom and me, as the three selected jumps were raised for the jump-off. 'It would only be wrong. I'll leave you both to Fate and your own good sense.'

The three selected jumps were the gate, the wall, and the triple.

'I haven't a chance, really,' said Tom.

'That's no way to look at it,' said Phil, shocked.

'Oh, let him look at it any way he likes, if it helps him,' cried Mary.

Lolly who was gazing at her brother with popping eyes, said, 'If you get another clear round, Tom, you can have my big china pony, and first go at our grooming tools for ever and ever.'

In order to end your agonising suspense, I will tell you that Janet Hare jumped a clear round, a girl called Angel Breeze from another team also did, and the two other competitors got four faults each. Then it was Tom's turn. He took the gate and the wall rather dashingly, and when he got to the triple took off too far away, jumped short, and got two faults.

As for myself, I soon realised that Plum was dying to do the jumps again. She was the perfect pony, and I owed everything to her. To feel her whisking over the jumps was heavenly, and no credit to me. She took the raised triple as if it were the easiest thing in the world, and I had got a second clear round.

Janet, Angel and I jumped off for the final decision, and I got the only clear round, with Janet second and Angel third. This put Tom in fourth place, and he got the allowance of marks and the green rosette and I was delighted for him.

When I came out, people started congratulating me – some of them perfect strangers – and I felt very embarrassed because Plum had done it all.

Amanda slapped me on the back, nearly breaking my spine, and said, 'Jolly good show!' and to her eternal sportsmanlike credit she never once said, 'Don't forget you were riding *my* pony.' I thought it was terribly decent of her, and that there was good in Amanda which would one day make her a frightfully nice person.

'Now we only have to wait for the final marks,' said Mrs Lockett, and we all groaned and said, 'Gosh, I can't bear it.'

We had to wait twenty minutes, and when the President of the Show, Sir Somebody Something, came out to the table in front of the grandstand, in all that enormous crowd on the stands and round the rails, you could have heard a feather drop, never mind a pin.

Even then he didn't announce the result, but kept everybody in agony by making a speech about the aims and objects of the competition, the value of the team spirit, and sportsmanship in general, which everybody knew about in any case.

He then picked up the fateful piece of paper, and put his glasses on and took them off again about four times.

'I now have much pleasure in declaring the result of today's Team Show,' he said, 'in which nobody gets prizes or individual marks, but all have worked for their team. The results are as follows: third place, Valley Farm Team with 159 points; second place, the Rectory Team with 168 points; and first and winners of the Cup, the Locketts' Team with 170 points.'

We just couldn't make a sound, we looked at each other dumbly, hardly hearing the cheers. Then we rode in, in three pairs, Mary and I leading, Jane and Lolly behind us, and the two boys at the rear.

'Lolly's to take the Cup,' said Mary. 'She's the youngest and she did jolly well and got us all those bonus marks.'

So Lolly went up for the big silver Cup, her face scarlet, and her riding hat slithering over one eye, and no dignity but a grin from ear to ear, and the crowd adored her and yelled like mad, and what do you think she did? She put one arm round the Cup because it was too heavy to hold in her hands, and the other arm round Sir Somebody Something, and she actually gave him a kiss! And he loved it, and laughed like anything, and so did everybody else; and then Phil went up and got the prize money, as did the other two teams, and we rode round the ring and felt terrific.

'Nice work,' said Mrs Lockett gruffly when we got back. 'Nice work, kids. And now let's come down to earth and look after those ponies, because they must be jolly tired.'

15   Friends all round

'I say, I wouldn't mind being asked back by you lot for supper,' said Amanda Applewood, 'as I'm staying with some frightfully dull people.'

'Come by all means,' said Mrs Lockett. 'After all, Plum is your pony.'

We all began to laugh, and I said, 'Oh dear, I shall be sorry to part with her, because she's been marvellous, but it'll be heavenly to see my own two ponies again and I wouldn't swop them.'

Then, of course, the others all began to ask me about my ponies, and as you who have read my previous books know, I can talk about Black Boy and Rapide for ever.

When we got back home we all went a bit mad. We did a sort of ballet while we fed and rubbed down the happy, clever ponies, and put them up for the night, and we all fell over each other and laughed like anything, and if you had seen Jane and Phil trying to do the *pas de deux* from Swan Lake you would have rolled on the ground.

Then we rushed upstairs and had baths and changed and came down to supper. *What* a supper! Mrs Lockett had laid on everything, regardless of stripping the larder, and as the news of our fame had spread round the neighbours, somebody had sent in sausage rolls and somebody else a trifle and a big iced cake.

You should have seen Amanda's face! 'And to think I didn't want to come here!' she said.

'It hasn't been like this all the time,' said Mary solemnly. 'Nothing but hard work, and bread and margarine to eat, Jill can tell you that.' She winked at me, and I added, 'And not even margarine always.'

The Cup stood gleaming on the sideboard, and Mrs Lockett said, 'This is an outright win, a once-and-once-only, and we shall hold this cup for ever, so you people will have to make a rota for cleaning it and keeping it shining like it is now. Between you you won it, but don't ever let that make you conceited, though you deserve to be proud – you're old enough to know the difference; and don't ever get the idea that you're marvellous or that you know everything about riding, because you never will. When you look at this Cup, remember that you're sportsmen and sportswomen, and never let your side down, or British sportsmanship either. And that's the end of my little sermon. Amen.'

Everybody clapped, and I suddenly felt a funny lump in my throat because I realised that it would never be my turn to clean the Cup. It was all over, I was about to say goodbye to the Locketts and go home, after a fortnight that began rather queerly but had turned out to be one of the happiest of my life.

'I expect I'd better see about going home tomorrow,' I said.

'Oh, no,' they all cried. 'You must stay till Tuesday, Jill because we're going to have a car picnic for a treat.'

So I said I would stay.

We sat over the supper table for ages, talking over every single event of the Show, what we had done and what we hadn't done and what we wished we had done, and living the whole day again, especially the winning bits.

'And there's this cheque for two hundred and fifty pounds,' said Phil. 'Will you cash it for us on Monday, Father, and then we can divide it out?'

'I never dreamed of so much money,' said Mary. 'Forty-one pounds each, and *still* four pounds over. Phil and Jane and I have decided to spend half of our shares on stable equipment and then we'll have something jolly good and useful for the ponies for another season.'

'Lolly and I are going to save half ours,' said Tom, 'until we need something for the ponies, and we're going to spend the other half on things we want now, like super skates.'

'I'm going to spend mine on my ponies,' I said, 'but I don't know just how. To think of going home with forty-one pounds!'

'I was just wondering,' said Mr Lockett, 'about that four pounds over. Would you like to do a little competition – no prizes? Just for fun, would you all write down on a slip of paper what you think is a good way of spending it? It'll be interesting, all your different points of view. Look, I've got some slips ready. Take one each.'

This intrigued us, and we all reached out for the slips, and went into huddles over them. Actually the huddles only lasted about a minute. Everybody wrote quite quickly and firmly, and then folded their slips and passed them back to Mr Lockett.

'That was jolly quick!' he commented. 'I wonder what we've got.'

He opened all the six slips – because of course Amanda hadn't voted, not being one of those concerned – and a look of wonder came over his face.

'This is really most amusing,' he said. 'And very satisfactory. Just let me read these aloud, one after the other.'

He began to read each slip in turn. ' "Buy Mother a present for coaching us" . . . "A present for Mother for coaching us" . . . "A nice present for Mrs Lockett for taking so much trouble coaching us" ' – that was mine – ' "A present for Aunt Phyllis for being our coach" . . . "Buy Aunt Phyllis something nice for coaching us" . . . "Mother deserves the four pounds for coaching us".'

He looked at Mrs Lockett, and you should have seen her face!

Everybody shouted 'Hurray' and Mary said, 'Oh Mother, what would you like?'

'Nothing,' said Mrs Lockett, but she looked terribly pleased.

'I know what she wants,' shouted Jane. 'A yellow scarf, and there's a smashing one in Mowbray's shop for three pounds seventy-five, and she can have the other twenty pence in a chocolate bar, and I vote we go and get it first thing Monday morning.'

Everybody cheered, including Amanda.

Next morning she took Plum away with her in a horse box and when I said goodbye to that lovely pony I felt quite sad, and I think Plum did too because she must have got a bit fond of me.

'What's the fuss?' said Amanda. 'You can come and ride her any time.'

We had a wonderful car picnic and Mrs Lockett wore the new yellow scarf which we had rushed into town to buy. On the Tuesday morning I went home by train, having learned that Mummy had already arrived back at our cottage from London. The whole family came to the station to see me off.

'Oh, I do wish you'd come to Chatton and see me and my ponies some day,' I cried.

'That's a rash invitation,' said Mary, laughing. 'We'd be like an invasion. But we've already decided that you're coming to stay with us again before many more hols have passed, and we'll ask Amanda too, and then we'll have both the Amandas at once. That'll be something!'

As soon as I got home Mummy said, 'Now where have you been? I've been smelling a mystery for some time. What's been happening?'

We sat down to lunch, and I told her the whole story from beginning to end. It took ages, especially as I was trying to do justice to the roast lamb and green peas while I talked.

'I suppose I ought to realise by now,' said Mummy, 'that you'll spend the rest of your life having adventures. There's no end to them.'

'As long as there are ponies in them,' I said, 'I don't mind how many adventures I have. Somehow when you've got ponies you always have adventures. And out of this one I've made six new friends, not counting grown-up ones.'

'Six?' said Mummy. 'I thought there were only five Locketts?'

'There's Amanda,' I said firmly. 'I've simply got to count Amanda.'

And thinking of Amanda I laughed like anything.